JESSICA BECK
THE DONUT MYSTERIES, BOOK 54
WICKED WEDDING DONUTS

S0-BBM-180

The First Time Ever Published!
The 54th Donuts Mystery!
Wicked Wedding Donuts

Jessica Beck is the *New York Times* Bestselling Author of the Donut Mysteries, the Cast Iron Cooking Mysteries, the Classic Diner Mysteries, and the Ghost Cat Cozy Mysteries.

NOT ONLY DOES GABBY Williams reopen ReNEWed beside Donut Hearts, but she also holds a surprise wedding. The best man couldn't make it due to a car accident, and soon after the nuptials, the groom is struck down with poison. Suzanne and Grace must figure out what really happened before their friend becomes either the number-one suspect in the poisoning, or maybe even the next victim!

This one's for all of you Donut Shop readers out there.
I couldn't, and wouldn't, do this without you all, each and every one of you!
And as always,
To P and E.

Chapter 1

THE TRUTH OF THE MATTER is that there's not much I *don't* love about weddings, but I do usually prefer a little notice before the actual ceremony takes place. After all, how else can I possibly get a suitable gift for the newly betrothed couple?

Honestly though, I wasn't the only one caught off guard in April Springs, North Carolina, by what happened. The fact that it took place during the grand reopening of ReNEWed—the gently used clothing shop Gabby Williams was relaunching next door to Donut Hearts—and that I got a bit more warning than most folks didn't help matters, either.

And then to top things off, there was an attempted murder before the ink on the marriage license even had a chance to dry, and I was called into action to find the would-be killer before *both* spouses had a very short "til death do us part" indeed.

But I'm getting ahead of myself. I do that sometimes. My name is Suzanne Hart, I make donuts for a living, and every now and then, I solve a murder or two as well.

Chapter 2

"SUZANNE, I HAVE A FAVOR I need to ask of you," Gabby Williams said when she walked into Donut Hearts, my shop that was located beside her new/old business, ReNEWed. It had been an arduous process getting the place rebuilt after a fire that had nearly killed the woman, but she'd persevered nonetheless, and the day of the Grand Reopening had finally arrived upon us.

"Gabby, I already came in early this morning and made *fourteen* dozen donuts just for the celebration, and you know just what 'early' means when I say it. I've been here since well before two a.m. Don't tell me you're canceling your order."

She frowned for a second before she replied, "No, of course not. Suzanne, I would never do that to you."

"Then you want eight dozen more, is that it? I'm sorry, but I just can't do it," I said, trying to head things off while I still could. Gabby and I were friends, much to my continuing surprise, but there were some things that I wouldn't do even for her.

"Would you please just take a deep breath and let me get a word in edgewise?" Gabby asked, sounding much calmer than she normally did. I couldn't understand it. She'd gone through some real labor pains getting her shop back, a true phoenix rising from the ashes, and she'd been a royal pain to all of us around her in the process. So where had she suddenly found so much calm?

"Are you on medication or something?" I asked her as I studied her pupils to see if they were dilated, wondering if that was the source of her serenity.

"I take something for my high blood pressure, and something else for my gout," she said. "Why do you ask?"

"Are either one of those pills mood altering?" I asked her. There was no point beating around the bush. Gabby was definitely a "shoot-from-the-hip" kind of woman, and I'd found that it suited me better when I didn't dance too delicately around her, either.

Instead of blowing up as I suspected she might, Gabby just grinned at me. "I'm happy. Don't you recognize a smile when you see one?"

"Honestly, it's not there enough for me to know it very well," I answered her plainly. "You really *are* happy about ReNEWed reopening, aren't you?"

"I am," she said levelly, "but that's not the reason I'm smiling right now." She lowered her voice a bit before she asked me, "Suzanne, can you keep a secret?"

"If you have to ask, then maybe you shouldn't tell me," I advised her.

"Of course you can," Gabby said dismissively. She looked around my donut shop and saw a few stragglers still sitting at one of the couches near the window. I was set to close at eleven, my regular time, and Emma—my assistant—and I were supposed to start taking the donuts we'd made next door, so the lack of clientele didn't really disturb me all that much. Gabby waved a hand in the air. "Can you close a bit early as a special favor to me? I don't want anyone else to hear this."

This had to be staggering news for Gabby to ask me to do that. She took great pride in the fact that as women, we both ran businesses in town, and she wouldn't ask me to shut down unless it was important.

"Usually I wouldn't do it, but since today is so special, I'll close up early for you," I told her.

"It's more special than you realize," Gabby answered with a cryptic grin.

I walked over to the occupied couch and said, "Gentlemen, we're closing a bit early because of the festivities next door."

"But I'm not full yet," Nathan protested. He owned the sporting goods shop in town, and every now and then, he'd been known to sneak down and grab a donut when business got slow.

"If you can restrain yourself for half an hour, Gabby will be giving my donuts away for *free* right next door," I told him.

Nathan was notoriously cheap, so I'd known how to appeal to his nature. "Free? I'll see you over there."

As he and the two men he'd been eating with walked toward the door, Gabby said, "Remember, two donuts per customer at my opening, boys."

"Two sounds about right to me," Nathan said as he grinned and patted his stomach.

Once they were gone, I locked the door. "Okay, you've got my undivided attention, Gabby."

"What about Emma?" she asked. "Can't she start setting up next door?"

"Fine," I answered, willing to cater to *most* of her whims today but getting a bit exasperated nonetheless. I found my assistant in the kitchen, just finishing up the last stack of dirty dishes generated by our customer base.

"I closed early so we can start getting set up at Gabby's," I told her.

"Do you really need my help this afternoon?" she asked me.

"Let me guess. You either have a class or some restaurant-opening preparations to do," I said.

"As a matter of fact, I'm just not looking forward to being around Gabby all afternoon," she admitted.

I whispered, "Keep your voice down. She's out front, Emma."

"Ha ha ha. Very funny," my assistant said as she stuck her tongue out at me and walked out of the room saying mockingly, "Why, Gabby Williams, how good to see you."

"It's good to see you, too, Emma Blake," Gabby said.

I watched as Emma's mouth opened and then closed again, though nothing else made its way out. I suppose it could have gone a lot worse. She might have said something that we'd both end up regretting. "Congratulations," she added lamely.

Gabby shot me a quick look of concern. "Did you say anything to her, Suzanne?"

"She already *knows* about the festivities next door, Gabby," I told her. "Who do you think helped me make all of those donuts?"

"Oh, of course," Gabby answered, catching herself. She was acting oddly, and for Gabby, that was saying something.

"I'll just start running some of your donuts next door," Emma said as she ducked back into the kitchen and grabbed one of the carts we used for transporting large quantities of goodies. "Is the place unlocked, or do I need a key?"

"You won't need one. We're going to set your donuts up outside on the other side of ReNEWed, but I have a few tables for you to use inside the front door. Paige Hill is there seeing to things at the moment," Gabby said. "She'll let you in so you can get them."

"Paige closed her bookstore for you?" I asked. That really was asking a lot, since our businesses were run on razor-thin margins where every sale counted.

"Rita's covering things there at the moment," Gabby said. I knew that Paige's latest assistant, an older woman who loved working at The Last Page, didn't like to be there alone.

"I'll go get started, then," Emma said as she motioned for me to get the front door for her. "This is closer. Besides, I don't want to leave the back wide open," she added.

"I don't, either," I said. "I told you so," I added softly as she walked past me.

"What can I say? I didn't believe you," she answered just as softly.

Once Emma was gone, Gabby asked, "What did you just say to her that she didn't believe, Suzanne?"

"That you were in a good mood today when you had no right to be because of all the stress entailed in reopening your shop," I answered. It wasn't anywhere close to the truth, but I wasn't about to tell her what we'd really been discussing.

"That's the thing, though. It's not *just* the Grand Reopening," Gabby said with that odd smile again.

"Then what is it? We're all alone, just like you wanted. What is it that you wanted to tell me?"

"Suzanne, I'm getting married," she said. "Today," she added, almost as an afterthought.

"You're *what*?" I asked her in disbelief.

"Don't look so surprised," Gabby answered in response to my reaction. "I may seem old and over the hill to you, but I'm still a vibrant woman with plenty of life to live still ahead of me."

"I know that," I said, though I would never have described her situation that way in a million years. "I just didn't realize things were that serious with your mystery beau." Without even thinking about the consequences, I asked the obvious question, at least to me. "Gabby, does *he* know he's getting married today?"

Wow, could that have gone wrong so many ways. It was a good thing Gabby was so happy. "Of course he does. He proposed last night, and I accepted."

"What about all of the paperwork you need to get married?" I asked her.

"I have connections in City Hall," she said proudly. "The license was expedited this morning, and the mayor himself is going to perform the ceremony."

"Then I suppose congratulations are in order," I said, still not quite believing it.

"You should know better than that. You *never* congratulate the bride, Suzanne. You offer her your best wishes," Gabby corrected me. After all, she was in a good mood; she wasn't comatose.

"So, who's the lucky man?" I asked, holding my breath, hoping it was a union I could approve of, not that Gabby was there asking me for my permission.

"It's Harper Wilcox," she answered proudly.

Maybe I should have defied tradition and congratulated her after all. According to scuttlebutt, Harper Wilcox was a very rich, charming, and distinguished older man, one that a great many women in ten counties had set their sights for and had failed.

And Gabby, my very own crusty and abrasive Gabby, had been the one who'd finally won his heart.

It would have been rude to ask her how she'd done it, but it was certainly the biggest question I had on my mind the second I'd heard the news.

At least I was smart enough to keep it to myself, though.

"I know it might strike some folks as odd that we're doing this so quickly, but as you so delicately pointed out earlier, we're not getting any younger."

"I said nothing of the sort," I protested. Sure, I'd thought it, but I hadn't actually *said* it.

"You thought it, though," Gabby said, shaking her head slightly as she spoke, "and don't bother denying it."

I couldn't very well do that, since I really did hate lying to my friends.

"All I can say is that if you're happy, I'm happy," I told her, and that much was one hundred percent true.

"I knew you'd feel that way. Suzanne, would you do me the privilege of standing next to me when I exchange vows with Harper? I want you to be my maid of honor."

I wasn't sure how many shocks my system could take, but apparently, I was about to find out. "Of course I will, but are you sure you wouldn't want one of your other friends?"

"I might, but they are all either visiting family, on vacation, or dead," Gabby said without an ounce of irony in her voice. "You're the best friend I could come up with on the spur of the moment."

I'd had more flattering compliments in my life, but I wasn't about to point that out. "I'd be honored, then," I told her. "What do I have to do?"

"Stand beside me when I tell you to, take my bouquet, and then hand me Harper's ring when I ask for it. It's simple," she said. "Oh, and you can't tell anybody. We want it to be a surprise."

"I'll do my best."

Then, to my surprise, Gabby hugged me. It wasn't just a gentle, one-off embrace either. She nearly cracked my ribs, she hugged me so hard. "Suzanne, I am so very happy I could split in half!"

I'd never heard that particular expression before, but it certainly suited her. Gabby was clearly overjoyed by the prospect of her impending nuptials.

It was a shame her joy would be so short lived, but neither one of us knew that at the time.

Chapter 3

"EMMA, WHY DON'T YOU go grab the last bunch of boxes while I work on the table arrangement?" I asked my assistant when I arrived on the scene. She'd gotten the tables from Paige and had set them up in front of the long-defunct Patty Cakes shop, a vacant storefront on Springs Drive. I knew that Emma wasn't thrilled about being around Gabby even if the crusty woman was sending out smiles instead of scowls at the moment, so I wanted to give her at least a moment's respite.

"Thanks. To be honest with you, it kind of creeps me out the way she keeps grinning at me. Is she drunk or something?"

"Just high on life, I suppose," I told her.

"If you say so," Emma conceded, though it was clear she didn't quite believe it. "Thanks for giving me a break," she added softly.

"You bet. I'm a great boss, right?" I asked her with a grin.

"Well, if you were *great*, you wouldn't make me come back," she replied with a soft smile of her own.

"Okay then, I'm still at least pretty good. You have to admit that much."

Emma laughed at that, and I joined her. "Fine, you're very good. I'll see you soon."

"I'll be right here when you get back."

"I'd like one donut, please," a woman said in a falsely deep voice behind me.

I knew it was Paige Hill without even turning around. "Swap me a donut for a book and you've got yourself a deal," I told her as I turned and grinned at her.

"Be careful what you offer. I got some real stinkers in a few days ago. I wouldn't push them on my worst enemy, let alone you." She surveyed what I'd done so far. "How many donuts did Gabby order for this?"

"More than she's ever going to need," I admitted.

"I hope you are at least charging her full retail for them."

I wasn't about to tell the truth, that I'd slashed my prices ridiculously low out of a sense of friendship. "Let's just say that I'm not hurting."

"Suzanne, do you know what your problem is? You're too nice."

"Yes, I hear that all the time, Paige. I could say the same thing about you, you know," I told her.

"What do you mean?"

"You left Rita in charge of The Last Page so you could help Gabby out. I know you're not getting any book sales from this, so face it. You're nice, too."

She looked around as though I'd said something offensive and replied softly, "Shh. I don't want it getting around." Paige added, "Where did Emma go? Did you cut her loose for the day?"

"I probably should," I said, starting to feel a bit guilty about keeping her so long. "She started working with me at two this morning to get all of these donuts finished in time."

"That's the glamorous life of a donutmaker, isn't it?" she asked.

"Oh, yes, it's nothing but Caribbean vacations and movie premieres for us," I told her, laughing.

Gabby walked over to us and frowned back toward her shop. "Paige, have you seen...never mind. There he is." George Morris had just walked onto the scene, and Gabby made a beeline for him without another word to either one of us.

"Why is she so eager to speak to the mayor?" Paige asked me.

I swear I didn't flinch, though I may have hesitated a split second before I answered. "He's making a speech and cutting the ribbon, isn't he?"

Most people would have never caught my hesitation, but my friend, Paige, was not most people. A lifetime of reading mysteries, added to the fact that we were close, had made her too aware of my usual behaviors and mannerisms. "Suzanne, what is it that you're not telling me?"

"Me? I wouldn't keep anything from you," I said, doing my best to sound sincere.

I must have failed at it miserably. "Come on, give."

Lowering my voice, I said, "I would if I could, but I can't."

"Can't or won't?" she asked me carefully.

"I gave Gabby my word," I told her.

Paige nodded. "That's all you had to say. I won't press you any harder."

"Thank you," I said gratefully.

"It's fine," she replied. "Just tell me this. Is it a long-term secret or a short-term one? Or would that be too revealing an answer?"

"I suppose if I had to say, it would be short term," I admitted, "but you didn't hear that from me."

"Hear what from you?" she asked me with a knowing smile.

"All I'll say is that if you can spare the time, you might want to hang around after the ribbon-cutting ceremony," I told her.

"Why? What's happening then?" she asked. "Never mind. Pretend I didn't ask you that. Mum's the word, Suzanne. I was planning to head over to the bookstore in a few minutes, but Rita will be okay on her own for a little longer. Will you save me a seat for the great unveiling?"

"I would if I could, but I can't," I said.

"Wow, when you keep a secret, you really keep a secret," she said just as Grace walked over and joined us. These two ladies were my best friends in the world, one of them since childhood and the other a lot more recently than that, but I loved them both.

"Is there something Suzanne won't tell you, Paige?" Grace asked. "I can make her talk, but it won't be pretty."

"No fair," I told her. "You can't tickle me to get me to tell you."

"Who says I can't?" Grace asked me with a slight smile. She was decked out in her regular business attire, a tailored suit that highlighted her svelte figure beautifully. I suppose I was in my business attire as well, even though it was just an old pair of jeans and a faded T-shirt. Blast it,

I needed to change before the ceremony! I wasn't going to stand up in front of half of April Springs looking like some kind of hillbilly hobo on Gabby's wedding day. "Grace, Paige, can you two do me a huge favor and finish this up? There's something I've got to do."

"No worries. We've got it covered," Paige said, and then she turned to Grace. "Right?"

"Right," she answered.

I dashed off toward the cottage, ducking behind Gabby and the mayor on my way, as well as avoiding a dozen folks who clearly wanted me to stop and chat. I didn't have time for that, and I surely didn't want to have to explain what I was doing, and more importantly, *why* I was rushing off at the last second.

"You look amazing," I told Jake as I rushed into the cottage and found him standing there tying his tie. He was wearing one of his old suits from the days when he'd been a state police investigator. The jacket and tie looked incredible on him, and the last time I could remember he'd gotten so dressed up was when he'd taken me to Napoli's in Union Square for one of our date nights recently.

"What can I say? I can clean up pretty good if I want to," he said with a smile. He frowned as he added, "Aren't you supposed to be helping Gabby at her grand reopening about now, Suzanne?"

I'd promised the bride-to-be that I wouldn't tell a soul about her news, and I'd meant it at the time, but I wasn't sure I could keep it from my husband.

"I wanted to grab a quick shower and change first," I said, which was true enough.

"For the wedding, not the reopening though, right?"

I frowned at him. "You already knew? It was supposed to be some kind of state secret. I'm going to kill Gabby."

"Don't," he said quickly. "She didn't say a word to me about it."

"Then how did you know?" I asked as I raced toward our bathroom, shedding clothes with every step, and then I jumped in the shower.

My husband followed close behind, as I knew he would. "I know the groom," Jake said. "He knew I lived in April Springs, so he came by and asked me to come."

"How do you know Harper Wilcox?" I asked him as I shampooed my hair.

"I did some work for him a few months ago," Jake admitted.

"I didn't know that."

"Suzanne, he asked me to keep it quiet, so I didn't feel as though I could talk about it. Sorry I didn't share it with you."

"No, that's fine. I get it," I told him. I knew that much of Jake's work was done in confidence. After all, if his clients, even the outside police forces who hired him, couldn't count on his discretion, then his consulting business didn't stand a chance. "Gabby asked me to be her maid of honor. Can you believe that?" I asked as I started toweling off. I wrapped my hair in another towel and hurried to my closet. I didn't have many nice things, at least not what the rest of the world would call nice, but what I did have I'd bought from Gabby. It was kind of fitting that I would be wearing something from her shop on her wedding day. "What do you think about this outfit?" I asked as I held up a floral print dress that came just above the knee that I really liked.

"You wore that on our last date night," Jake reminded me.

"Well, it's only fair. After all, you wore that suit."

"I love it," Jake said with a wry smile.

"Do you think it's appropriate, given the circumstances?"

"Well, you can't wear your fancy black dress, or your white one either, so why not go with that one?" Jake asked.

"So, you don't think I look good in it, is that what you're saying?" I asked him, pouting a bit. I didn't need a lot of positive reinforcement, but like anyone, I enjoyed a little.

"Suzanne, you'd look good to me in a trash bag. As a matter of fact, I like what you're wearing right now best of all," he said with a grin.

"You mean just a towel?" I asked with an uncharacteristic giggle.

"If that," he answered.

"You're forgiven," I told him as I started getting dressed rapidly.

"I didn't even know I was in the doghouse," he told me.

"I know. It's tough being you sometimes, isn't it?" I asked him with a grin.

"It has his benefits," Jake answered as he tried to hug me in my underwear.

"No, sir. There's no time for that," I reminded him.

"Suzanne, there's *always* time for that," he replied.

I just laughed as I finished getting dressed. "Let's go," I said as I grabbed a handbag, something I rarely carried.

"Okay, but there's something I need to tell you first," he said in dead seriousness.

"What is it?" I asked him, taken aback by the sudden serious tone of his voice.

"You. Look. Amazing."

"You are a sweet man and a good husband," I told him. "Thank you. Now let's go. I don't want to be late."

"Hey, they can't have the wedding without the maid of honor," Jake said with a laugh.

"Knowing Gabby, I'm not even sure not having George Morris there could stop her. She seems bound and determined to get married, and I mean right this minute. Why the rush, do you think?"

Jake frowned for a moment as we left the cottage and raced across the park, taking a shortcut to the festivities. "I can't say."

"Does that mean you don't know, or you're not allowed to tell me?" I asked him.

"I can't say," he repeated.

"Got it," I replied.

As we neared ReNEWed and the crowd of people standing around, Jake said, "I've got to talk to Stephen Grant about something. I'll catch up with you later."

"What do you have to talk to the chief of police about that can't wait?" I asked him.

He just winked at me, and knowing that was all the answer I was going to get, I winked back. As I headed to the tables now filled with my donuts, I found Emma finishing up. "What happened to Grace and Paige?"

"They took off when I got back," she said. "They wanted me to tell you that they did the best they could but that they were leaving the last-minute touches to the pros."

"That's fine with me," I answered. "You didn't even need me. Everything looks great," I said as I took in the tables. I loved seeing my donuts spread out and featured in all of their glory, especially since they'd be serving as wedding donuts for the ceremony. I'd catered more than one wedding in the past where the bride and groom preferred my treats to traditional wedding cake, and it always made me feel good inside. After all, who didn't like donuts? Nobody *I* cared to know, that was for sure.

"Suzanne, where's your husband?" George Morris asked me as he approached.

"He was searching for Chief Grant the last time I saw him," I told him. "Why the worried look, Mr. Mayor?"

"Someone needs to speak with him," George said.

"Can you possibly be a bit *more* vague than that?" I asked him.

He motioned me away from Emma, and I took a few steps back so we'd have a bit more privacy, not that anyone there was paying any attention to us.

"This is serious. I need to find your husband, ASAP," he said.

"What's going on, George?"

"Harper's best man was in a car accident on his way over here a little while ago," George explained. "He got pretty banged up in the wreck, so he's not going to be able to make it to the ceremony."

"That's terrible," I answered. "What do you need Jake for, though?"

"Harper wants him to stand in as his best man. We've got three minutes before my speech, and then the wedding is set to take place, so we need to find Jake fast."

"Well, you can both rest easy, because he's right here," my husband said as he walked up behind us. "I don't ordinarily refer to myself in the third person, and now I know why. What's up, George?"

"Harper's looking for you. He's got a favor to ask."

"He already found me," Jake said. "It looks like I'll be standing up there with you, Suzanne."

"I can't think of a single place I'd rather you be," I told him. Talking to both men, I lowered my voice as I added, "Is it just me, or is this whole thing a little crazy?"

"Coming from anyone else, I'd agree," George said, "but seeing how it's Gabby Williams, I'm not surprised a bit. The only thing that caught me off guard was the bridegroom's identity. I'm not entirely sure how that match is going to work out in the long run." He frowned before he added, "Suzanne, I know you and Gabby are friends. I didn't mean anything by that. It's just not an obvious match, you know what I mean?"

"Relax, George, I'm as puzzled by it as you are. Oh, well. That's life."

Gabby came over, and she'd changed as well. I hadn't expected her to wear white, and she hadn't disappointed me, but she was in a designer peach-toned dress that fit her beautifully, one that accentuated every curve and line. "Gabby, you look incredible," I told her.

She smiled for a second before she replied, "I've been saving this dress for years for a special occasion." She then turned to Jake and barked out, "Harper's looking for you."

"He already found me," my husband said lightly.

"Well, he wants you again. He's in my office. Go," Gabby commanded, and my husband did as he was told, but not before pausing to kiss her cheek gently.

"Wow. I mean wow. You look incredible."

She grinned, and I could swear I saw her blush a bit. Gabby chose the oddest times to act human, and it never failed to catch me by surprise.

"I sold you that dress," Gabby said accusingly as she turned back to me.

"You did. How does it look?"

She frowned for a moment before she spoke. "Suzanne, you're not trying to outshine the bride, are you?"

"Gabby, that couldn't happen on my best day. My husband was right. You are a knockout, lady."

"Thank you." She then turned to George. "Are you ready to get this thing started?"

"The reopening or the wedding?" the mayor asked her.

"Both," Gabby replied. "As soon as you cut the ribbon, make the announcement. Harper knows his cue, so he and Jake will come up and join us then."

"Sounds good to me," the mayor said.

Gabby paused. "Aren't *you* going to tell me how good I look, too?" she asked him critically.

"Why should I? You own a mirror, don't you?" George asked with a shrug.

"That's why I like you, Mr. Mayor. You're more like me than you care to admit," Gabby answered. "Let's go, people. We've got a reopening and a wedding to put on!"

Chapter 4

"GREETINGS, EVERYONE," George Morris said as he stood in front of the resurrected building housing Gabby's gently used clothing store. "It is with great pleasure that I welcome you all to the Grand Reopening of ReNEWed, a shop that's been a cornerstone of April Springs for more years than anyone here cares to admit to."

As he paused for the chuckles from the crowd, I thought about how far the former cop, and my amateur investigating assistant, had come since he'd first been elected to his current position. George had blossomed in the job, developing and growing in more ways than any of us could ever have predicted. As he went on extolling Gabby's virtues, I found myself looking around the crowd. There were many folks I knew, mostly friends, with a few others who weren't so nice thrown in as well. I knew that some of the people there were not great pals of Gabby's either, so why had *they* come? Could it be they were just that excited about the prospect of getting free donuts? I didn't think so, but you never knew. Jake was off to one side with Harper, so Grace made her way to stand beside me.

"Are you seriously not going to tell me what's going on, Suzanne?" she asked.

"If you wait five minutes, I won't have to," I told her in a whisper. "Now shh. I want to hear the mayor's talk."

"Suzanne Hart, don't you dare shush me."

"Sorry," I amended quickly.

"You're a part of whatever's going to happen, so don't try to deny it." She was clearly a little miffed that I was keeping something from her. I'd promised Gabby I'd keep it to myself, but at what cost? I didn't want Grace upset with me, especially about something that would be common knowledge soon enough.

"Gabby's marrying Harper Wilcox right after the dedication," I told her softly.

"What?" Grace asked loudly just as the mayor was pausing for dramatic effect.

Everybody there, and I mean everybody, looked at her.

Grace at least had the decency to blush. "Sorry," she said quickly, and then she took a step backward, no doubt trying to blend in with the crowd.

George went on, and I glanced back at Grace and shook my head. "Smooth."

"I'm sorry," she said softly. "I just couldn't believe it. Harper Wilcox is quite the catch."

"So I've heard. Well, our Gabby caught him. That's the big surprise."

"She's not 'our' anything," Grace corrected me. "The woman hates me, and you know it."

"You two aren't best friends, but I wouldn't say that she hates you. There are other folks she reserves that for," I insisted. "That's just how Gabby is."

"Well, you two are certainly chummy enough. I can't believe she told you ahead of time."

I bit my lower lip a second before I answered. "Actually, I'm her maid of honor."

"Of course you are," Grace said as George wound up his speech. As the mayor turned backward, his latest in a long line of assistants, a woman named Kath Martin, handed him a gigantic pair of gold-plated scissors. I was kind of surprised that Gabby didn't say something to the crowd as well, but I had to believe that she was nervous about the upcoming nuptials.

"I now officially declare ReNEWed reopened for business," George said as he tried to cut the yellow ribbon stretched across the doorway.

The only problem was that the scissors didn't work.

No matter how many times he tried, they just wouldn't cut the tape.

So George, being George, told the crowd with a smile, "Hang on, folks. I can take care of this." He pulled out the multipurpose tool that was always on his hip these days and pulled out a small pair of scissors. With these, he cut the tape, and the audience cheered.

Gabby frowned for a moment, and then she smiled with the rest of the crowd as they started to surge forward.

"Before we all make our way to the free donuts and sodas as well as the wonderful clothes inside, there's one more item on the agenda," George said. "If you'll all bear with us for one second, we can get started on part two of today's festivities."

I stepped toward Gabby as Harper and Jake joined the mayor up front.

"Are you ready?" Gabby asked me softly. I had no idea how she'd managed to sneak up on me like that.

"I am if you are," I said.

"I've been ready for a very long time," she answered.

"Then let's go join my current husband and your future one," I said as I offered her my arm.

She took it as we made our way up front, and I was surprised to feel her shaking. "Gabby, are you okay?" I asked her.

"It's nothing that a little marriage won't take care of," she admitted.

"Then let's see if we can't make that happen," I told her.

"If everyone can stay right where you are, we've got another special treat for you today," George said, getting the crowd back under control with just the strength of his voice. "We are all gathered here today to witness the marriage of Gabrielle Celeste Williams and Harper Dillon Wilcox."

The crowd murmured among themselves, wondering if it was real, when Harper and Jake stepped up to the mayor. Gabby looked at me and nodded, and we joined them on the other side. She'd had the bouquet with her, so when she and Harper met in the middle, she stopped and handed the flowers to me. She'd given me the ring earlier, and I held it clenched in my free hand, since this particular dress didn't have any pockets. That was one of the reasons I preferred blue jeans. That, and the fact that it didn't matter if I got them covered in my donut detritus.

"As we witness the union of these two souls, let us all celebrate the love they feel for one another,\ and the promise that it brings," George said. I'd never heard him perform a wedding before, and I was amazed by how polished the man had become. He was amazing! As he continued with the exchange of vows between them, I glanced over at Jake, who was watching me instead of the happy couple. When he saw me looking at him, he winked at me and grinned, and I returned it in full. I was so happy that he'd come into my life, and to think it had all happened because of murder. It proved that even the darkest clouds had silver linings sometimes.

I was still musing about our first meeting when I noticed that George had stopped talking. Gabby looked at me, and through clenched teeth, she said, "The ring, Suzanne."

I handed it to her, trying not to make eye contact. As happy as Gabby was at the moment, I didn't want to see her scolding gaze.

Things went smoothly from there on, until George announced, "What we join here together, let no one put asunder. I now pronounce you husband and wife. You may kiss the bride."

"Or I can kiss the groom," Gabby said, grabbing Harper and pulling him in for a big kiss. The groom just laughed at the gesture, and the entire crowd applauded.

The happy couple went into ReNEWed as George said, "There are donuts for everyone over there, and coffee and soft drinks across the street, so help yourselves. We'll see the happy couple again very soon."

They must have prearranged their exit, and suddenly I saw that Emma was about to be stormed by the impromptu wedding guests, so I hurried over to join her, with Grace and Paige not far behind.

"What do we do?" Paige asked as everyone started pressing toward us.

"Put a donut on a napkin and hand it to someone," I told her as Emma and I started doing the same thing. One of Harper's acquaintances from Union Square had set up a coffee-and-soft-drink station on the other side of Springs Drive closer to Paige's bookstore, so at least that took some of the crowd away from us initially.

"What if they want a certain kind?" Grace asked.

"Tell them they'll have to learn to live with disappointment," I told her as I handed out more donuts. "They're free, so beggars can't be choosers."

"I can't wait to tell them that," Grace answered with a grin.

"Let's try not to start any riots, okay? Keep those donuts moving, ladies."

We handled the first rush of customers, and by the time I saw familiar faces coming back for seconds, we had things under control. Gabby and Harper came out and headed toward us, and there was a new wave of cheers, though quite a bit more subdued compared to when they'd exchanged vows.

"May I get the happy couple a donut apiece?" I asked them.

"We already had them in the changing area inside," Gabby said. "Thank you for providing them. I've been so nervous I haven't eaten all morning."

"I had two myself," Harper said with a grin. "Thanks, Suzanne."

"You're welcome," I told them. "But I can't take credit for thinking of it. Thank Emma."

"I didn't do it," my assistant said.

"Well, *whoever* thought of it, be sure to thank them for the donuts and the sodas," Gabby said. "We need to go over and thank Grady, too. He's supplying the drinks."

"We went to school together, so he owed me one," Harper chimed in, and then a look of discomfort crossed his face.

"Are you feeling okay, Harper?" I asked him.

"I'm fine. It must just be all of the excitement," he answered. "I'll be okay."

And then he collapsed right in front of us.

"Call 911," Gabby screamed as she fell to her new husband's side. "He's having convulsions!"

I'd seen Dr. Zoey Hicks in the crowd earlier. Didn't that woman ever work? Maybe this time it would be to our advantage. As I scanned the crowd, I couldn't see her, though. "Zoey Hicks!" I shouted. "Has anyone seen her?"

"She had to go back to the hospital," someone answered.

"Did he have a heart attack or something?" another person called out.

I looked down to see Gabby pulling Harper's tie loose so he could breathe easier, and she kept trying to put his head in her lap, but his body kept jerking uncontrollably. She tried her best to comfort him, and I saw her whispering to him when the paramedics cut through the crowd. It was Howie and Gert, two EMTs I trusted, pushing a wheeled stretcher like a battering ram through the group.

"Make a hole, people," Gert demanded, and the crowd parted as though she was brandishing a cattle prod.

When she got to Harper, she knelt down and started checking him as Howie lowered the stretcher. After a moment, she and Howie loaded Harper onto it, strapping him to the gurney after they moved him and then raising the stretcher to its full height again so they could get to him to their waiting ambulance.

"What's wrong with him?" Gabby cried out in anguish, and I felt my heart break for my friend. She deserved better than this. What a horrible wedding day!

She followed beside them as they made their way back to the ambulance, and after that, folks kept talking about what might have happened to the bridegroom.

"It was his heart," one person said. "He's had problems, you know."

"A heart attack doesn't send you into convulsions and make you stop breathing," another one said.

"What causes that?" the original person asked.

"Poison," the other said.

And then I remembered the donuts they'd both eaten so recently.

Had someone used one of my treats as a murder weapon yet again? It had happened before, and I'd prayed that I'd never have to deal with that again.

Chapter 5

"BOX THE REST OF THESE back up," I told the ladies the second I suspected what might have happened to Harper Wilcox.

"But we haven't gotten any yet," a pair of men protested as Grace and Emma had been about to hand them donuts.

"Sorry. We have to shut this down right now," I told them. "Tell you what. Come by Donut Hearts tomorrow morning and I'll give you each two donuts, on the house."

"How will you know it's us?" one of them asked me skeptically.

"I'll remember you," I told them. Then I said to Emma, Paige, and Grace quietly, "Nobody else gets a donut, understand?"

"Why not?" Grace asked as she did what I'd told her to do.

"I have my reasons," I said, not wanting to even say what I suspected may have happened out loud.

"Do you think someone poisoned one?" Paige asked me.

Unfortunately, one of the men I'd refused to serve heard her and said loudly, "The donuts are poisoned. Everybody, throw your donuts away!"

In an instant, there was bedlam. People were throwing their half-eaten donuts on the ground while others were trying to make themselves throw up what they'd just eaten. I had to put a stop to this, and fast.

"The donuts are fine!" I shouted, though I couldn't prove it. "You're all going to be just fine!"

"Did Harper Wilcox think that too before he took a bite of poison?" someone I didn't recognize shouted out.

"My donuts didn't do it," I said as confidently as I could muster.

"Suzanne, I'm so sorry," Paige said. "I feel awful."

"It's okay," I replied, though I knew that it wasn't. Once a rumor like that started spreading, it didn't matter if there was any basis in fact or not. In an hour. all of April Springs would believe that one of my treats had put Harper Wilcox in the hospital and maybe even caused something worse. It would take a long time to dispel that rumor, and I prayed that one of my donuts hadn't really done that to the bridegroom.

I couldn't be sure, though.

That was what made it so bad.

Grace must have been thinking the same thing that I had been. She grabbed a box we'd just filled, went up on the stage where the grand reopening and the wedding had been performed so recently, and she grabbed the live microphone.

"Everyone, listen to me," Grace said. Once she had their attention, she flipped open the box, selected a donut at random, and ate it for the entire gathering to see.

I wanted to stop her, but before I could, Paige leapt up to join her and took a big bite of one of my donuts as well. "That's the best donut I've ever had in my life."

Before I knew it, a great many of my friends were joining them and doing the same thing. Emma took a box and went onstage, handing out a few on the way.

What could I do? I grabbed a box myself and joined them. I grabbed a donut at random and took a bite so big that nearly half of it was gone.

It might not have been the smartest thing for Grace, Paige, and the rest of my friends to do, but I was determined that if something was going to happen to them, then it was going to happen to me, too.

Fortunately, nobody collapsed, went into convulsions, or even showed the slightest sign of distress, though a few folks looked a little green around the gills from practically swallowing their donuts whole.

"Are you finished with the dramatics?" Chief Stephen Grant asked me as the crowd finally started to disperse.

"Hey, blame your wife," I told him. "She started it."

"Yeah, sometimes her emotions get the better of her," he said proudly. "We need to break this little feeding frenzy up, though."

"*Was* it the donut?" I asked him, holding my breath until I heard his response.

"It's too soon to tell," he told me. "We've got the shop cordoned off until we can check things out."

"What do I do with all of these?" I asked him as I pointed to the remaining boxes of donuts we had yet to put out.

"Take them back to Donut Hearts and lock them up," he said. When I started to speak again, he added quickly, "Just to be on the safe side."

I nodded. It was the prudent thing to do. In fact, I'd been about to do exactly that when Paige had misspoken and blown the lid off of everything. "I'll take care of it," I told him.

Emma and I started loading up the remaining boxes, with Paige and Grace trailing just behind us. A few more folks wanted handouts once they realized that no one else was going into convulsions, but I had my orders.

"I can't believe *I* caused that," Paige said miserably after we unloaded the remaining boxes in the back of the kitchen, away from our active food prep area. "I really screwed up, Suzanne. I'm so sorry."

"Hey, don't beat yourself up about it," Grace told her gently.

"That's easy for you to say. You were a hero out there," she answered.

"We all were. After all, not all heroes wear capes," Grace answered with a smile, trying to break the tension.

It didn't work. "Suzanne, I hope you can forgive me someday," Paige said as she rushed out of the shop.

"I was just kidding around, trying to break the mood," Grace protested as she started to go after her.

"You stay here. I'll go," I told her.

I caught Paige heading to her shop.

"Will you give me a second to catch up?" I asked her, nearly out of breath. In my defense, it had been a very long and stressful day.

"Suzanne, I can't face you right now," she shouted over her shoulder.

"It wasn't your fault," I told her. Sure, she could have refrained from speculating out loud about my donuts being the cause of whatever had happened to Harper Wilcox, but the real villain here was the man who had broadcast the suspicion to the crowd.

I dearly hoped he came by Donut Hearts the next morning.

He was going to get something from me, but it wasn't going to be a free donut.

"Please. Just leave me alone," she said through her tears.

I had no choice as she ran into her bookstore. I turned back, only to find Jake standing there, watching the entire scene unfold.

"What was that all about?"

"Did you not see the riot earlier?" I asked him incredulously.

"Ha ha, very funny. There wasn't really a riot," he replied.

"That's what you think. Paige accidentally asked out loud if Harper might have been poisoned by one of my donuts, and some loudmouth shouted out that it was a fact, that all of my donuts were poisoned!"

"That's terrible," Jake answered.

"She felt bad about saying it the second it was past her lips," I explained.

"I'm not talking about Paige, I mean what the other guy did. Who was it?"

"I didn't recognize him. Maybe it was someone from Union Square," I wondered out loud.

"So what did you do?"

"I stood there like a statue and watched as Grace marched up to the microphone with a box of donuts in her hands. She ate one right there in front of everybody to prove they weren't tainted! Paige wasn't far behind her, and neither was Emma. What could I do? I grabbed another box and joined them. I'm proud to say that a lot of my regular customers came up too, and we all had at least one donut to show that they were safe. Thank goodness nobody else went into convulsions. Where were you when all of this was going on?"

"The chief asked me to go to the hospital with him to interview Harper, but he's unconscious, and then I had to meet up with an old friend from the state police," Jake admitted.

"How is Harper doing? Is he still alive?" I hated the thought of Gabby being widowed so soon after taking her wedding vows, let alone the fact that Harper's life was in real jeopardy, whether because of one of my donuts or not.

"It's not good, Suzanne. He's in intensive care," Jake said. "We tried to talk to Gabby, but she's a real mess, so the chief came back here, and I had my meeting."

"Should I go be with her?" I asked.

"No, they've given her something to settle her nerves, so she's not speaking to anyone. I need to get over to ReNEWed. I've got to talk to Stephen."

I touched my husband's arm lightly to stop him before he could go. "Jake," I said softly, "do you think it *might* have been one of my donuts?"

"If it was, someone did something to it *after* it left your hands at Donut Hearts," he told me. "I know that with all of my heart, and so does the rest of April Springs."

"I hope you're right," I said weakly.

"You can count on it." He paused, and I could tell there was something else he wanted to tell me. I just wasn't sure he had permission to say it.

"What is it? Can you tell me?" I asked him softly.

My husband looked around and saw that we were alone. "You didn't hear this from me, but the hospital believes that he *was* poisoned from all of the signs. They just don't know how it was administered or even what was used. I wish I had better news for you, but you may have to plan on some counterattacks to keep this from ruining the donut shop if the poison was administered on top of one of your treats. That's strictly between you and me though, do you understand?"

"I do," I said, subconsciously echoing the line used earlier to unite Gabby and Harper.

"Now I really do have to go," he replied, but not before kissing me on my forehead.

Wow. What a mess this had all turned out to be. I found myself hoping for Harper Wilcox's recovery, and not just for his sake and Gabby's. If it turned out that someone had used one of my donuts to poison him and he died from it, I might not be able to survive the fallout.

"Before you do, why were you meeting up with someone from the state police? Was it for business or pleasure?"

He frowned before he answered. "I'm not sure it's my place to tell you about that."

A sudden thought struck me. "You're not going back to work for them, are you?" I knew that there were times Jake missed his old job as an investigator, and I'd been dreading the thought of him returning to the force ever since he'd retired.

"No, it wasn't for me," Jake said.

"But it *was* about a job," I pushed.

"Suzanne, I can't talk about it."

I ignored his protest. "So, if it wasn't for you, it had to be for someone else. Who else might be qualified? George Morris? No, he's too old, and besides, he's happy being mayor. It's not Darby or Rick. Neither one of those young officers is in any hurry to move on from the April Springs police force." And then it hit me. "It's Stephen, isn't it?"

My husband frowned for a split second. "Drop it, okay? I'm not going to say."

"You don't have to. Never play poker with me, Jake. I can read you like a book. Does Grace know that Stephen is trying to get in with the state police?"

He wouldn't even answer. "Good-bye, Suzanne." It was clear he wasn't all that happy with me, but I'd felt as though I'd had to push him.

I'd scored a direct hit, and I knew it. The problem was, what should I do with the information? I knew for a fact that Grace wouldn't approve of her husband taking on an even more dangerous job in law enforcement than being our chief of police. That meant that she didn't know about it yet. After all, if he had told her, she would have told me, and I mean fast.

That didn't really leave me any options.

I needed to tell Grace myself. While I didn't have any hard facts, I had a basket full of suspicions, and she had a right to know, just in case I was right.

Chapter 6

"WE NEED TO TALK," I told Grace when I walked back into Donut Hearts.

"And on that note, I'm going to get out of here," Emma said as she glanced at her phone. "Is that okay, boss?"

"It's fine," I told her.

"What's so important that we need the shop to ourselves?" Grace asked me after Emma was gone. "Are you pregnant?"

"What? No. Are you?"

"No, ma'am. So, if it's not that earthshaking, what it is?"

"It's about your husband," I told her.

"He's okay, isn't he?" she asked me, concern flooding her face.

"Yes, of course he is, at least as far as I know," I told her.

"Then what has he gotten himself into this time?"

"I only have a suspicion, and if you want me to keep it to myself, I will," I told her.

"Fat chance of that happening after you've already baited the trap," she said. "Spill, Suzanne."

"Jake had a meeting with an old friend from the state police," I told her.

"And what does that have to do with my husband?"

"It was about a job, but it wasn't for Jake," I answered. "Has Stephen talked to you lately about joining the state police?"

"No. Well, sort of. He's mentioned it a few times, but I've managed to kill the idea every time he does. Why, is Jake actually going to bat for him?" She looked as angry as I'd seen her in years.

"Hang on. He was just doing what he thought was a favor for a friend," I explained.

"And you're defending them both going behind my back to make something happen that I'm completely against? Whose side are you on, Suzanne?"

"Yours, first, last and always," I told her. "Now calm down, take a deep breath, and let's talk about this."

"I'm going to talk, but it's not going to be calmly," she said as she headed for the door. "First I'm going to find my husband, and then I'm going to track yours down."

"You honestly can't blame Jake," I told her.

"I can and I do, and if you're not careful, you're going to be on my list, too." She stormed out of the donut shop, and as I started to go after her, she said loudly, "Don't. Just don't."

I knew better than to cross her at the moment. Why were all of my best friends suddenly running away from me? It was bad enough that Gabby's new husband was in the hospital, fighting for his life, on his wedding day, but now both Grace *and* Paige didn't want to see me.

Some days it just didn't seem as though it was worth the trouble getting out of bed.

I had a few dozen donuts left at the shop from our regular run that morning, but I didn't feel like playing Good Samaritan and giving them away, so I went in back of the shop and chucked them in the trash.

When I came back in, I walked through Donut Hearts, turning off lights and making sure that everything would be ready for me the next day. It was a routine I always enjoyed performing, and I grabbed the bag with my deposit in it and turned off the final light out front.

When I finished locking the door, I heard someone calling my name. Great. What was this about?

And then I saw that it was Momma and Phillip, two people who were *not* angry with me at the moment, which put them in the minority, considering that Paige, Grace, and even Jake weren't in any mood to see me.

Hey, at that point, I would take what I could get.

"Any chance you have any donuts left from the festivities?" Phillip asked me. "We skipped lunch," he added as he glanced at my mother, his wife.

"Phillip, I told you to order something larger than a snack while we were in Asheville," Momma reminded him.

"There wasn't anything else on the menu I wanted to eat," Phillip protested. "Dot, I'm a carnivore, and you know it. I still don't understand why you stopped at Nature's Meat-Free Table."

"It's called Nature's Magnificent Table, and you well know it," Momma corrected him. "I explained it to you before. Henrietta and I have been friends for decades. When she told me how excited she was about opening her restaurant in Asheville, I promised her we'd be among her first customers."

"That's all well and good. I don't mind a salad now and then, but not as a main course."

"Now you're just being recalcitrant," she said.

"What I am being is hungry," he replied. "Come on, Suzanne, you've got to help me out."

"I'm sorry. I just threw the extra donuts for the day away," I told him.

"Were they still boxed up?" Phillip asked hopefully.

"Don't. You. Dare." Momma said the words distinctly, and with a great deal of force behind her enunciations.

"It was great seeing you, Suzanne. If you need me, I'll be over at the Boxcar Grill, eating something entirely unhealthy for me." He smiled and waved at Momma as he hurried across the street.

My mother waited until he was safely out of earshot before she smiled at me and said, "You should have seen his face when he saw the menu. It was so tragic it was amusing. How was the Grand Reopening?"

"You're not going to believe what happened," I told her.

"Something melodramatic, no doubt, knowing our Gabby," Momma said.

"If you call someone trying to kill Harper Wilcox dramatic, then I guess you'd be right."

Momma looked at me to see if I was joking, and after a full second she realized that I was telling her the straight, unvarnished truth. "Why would someone try to kill Harper? What was he doing at the event, anyway?"

"Oh, that's the other thing," I told her. "He and Gabby got married."

"Now I *know* you're making it up," Momma told me, and once again, she locked her gaze with mine. "You're not, are you? They're really married?"

"They are," I told her.

"Oh, dear," Momma said.

"Why? Aren't you happy for Gabby?" I asked her.

Momma took a few seconds to collect herself, and then she waved a hand in the air. "Never mind about that. How is Harper? What did the assailant use as a weapon?"

"I'm not sure, but it may have been one of my donuts," I admitted. "He was poisoned."

"Oh, Suzanne," Momma said, her disappointment clear in her voice.

"It's not like we even know *how* it was administered yet," I explained. "It may have been something else entirely, like some coffee or soda he might have had, which I did not provide, by the way, in case that was about to be your next question."

"There's that, then. Tell me what happened, and don't leave out any of the details."

After I brought her up to speed on the reopening, the wedding, and the bridegroom's collapse at the reception, Momma just shook her head. "Gabby has certainly had her share of troubles over the years, hasn't she?"

"And the hits just keep on coming," I answered. "I hope Harper pulls through. They genuinely seem to care for one another." Something happened then that I had to ask her about. "Momma, every time I mention that man's name, you flinch a little. What do you know that I don't?"

"Do you honestly care to ask me such an open question, Suzanne? It begs a rude response, doesn't it?"

"Okay, you've got a point. What is it about Harper in particular that you're not telling me?"

She was about to reply when Geneva hurried up to us. Momma's assistant and I had buried the hatchet and had recently begun to form a friendship of sorts, but I didn't want her interrupting what my mother had been about to tell me. "Geneva, can this wait one second?"

"Of course," she said as she stepped back. "I'm so sorry." It was clear that I'd hurt her feelings.

"No, I'm the one who is sorry," I said quickly. "That was rude of me. Go on, tell Momma what you need to tell her. This can wait."

She looked from me to Momma and then back at me again. "Are you sure?"

"Geneva, report," Momma said, her command dripping with authority.

I felt my posture improving at the very tone in her voice, and it hadn't even been directed at me.

"It's Bethany Halstead. She wants to pull out of your deal, and nothing I say seems to get her attention."

"How about the fact that we have a signed contract?" Momma asked.

"She told me to tell you that if you wanted to get all formal about it, you could just go ahead and sue her. I'm sorry. I did everything in my power to convince her that she was legally bound by what she signed, but she refused to even listen to me. She told me that she wouldn't deal with a lowly underling who wasn't worth wasting her breath on and that she'd take it up with you and only you."

That last bit pained Geneva to convey; I could see it in her posture and her expression.

"We'll just see about that," Momma said before turning to me. "Suzanne, I do apologize, but we must continue this discussion later."

"As long as you're willing to revisit it soon," I told her. "Gabby's my friend."

"She is mine as well. I'll call you the moment I've had a chance to speak with Bethany." Momma turned back to Geneva, and as they walked toward Momma's car, she told her assistant, "I'm truly sorry she treated you so badly."

"It's okay," Geneva said, clearly happy that she wasn't taking the brunt of Momma's ire for delivering bad news.

"No, it's not, but we will correct it," Momma said as she squeezed Geneva's hand and smiled.

I loved my momma, but at that moment, I liked her too. That wasn't always easy to do, especially when she got so overprotective of me, but this wasn't one of those times.

I was standing there wondering what to do with myself when I realized that there was nothing I *could* do at the moment. Gabby was with her new husband at the hospital, Grace was on her own mission, and apparently, neither Paige nor Jake had any interest in speaking with me.

I had at least one good friend left in April Springs that I hadn't alienated yet, so I decided to go see her at the Boxcar Grill. I could use a friendly face, and at that moment, they were rare indeed.

"Hey, there," I told Trish Granger the moment I walked in. "How are you doing today?"

"I'm fine," Trish said as she swiveled her head toward me, sending her ever-present ponytail flying in the air. "I hear you've been having a tough day."

"Not as tough as some other folks," I answered.

"Yes, everyone's talking about Gabby's quick marriage and her sudden possible widowhood all in the same day."

"Is there news about Harper?" I asked her.

"No, at least not that I've heard," she explained. "Did some bozo actually shout out that your donut was what poisoned him?"

"Pretty much," I admitted.

"I heard the entire town had a donut to prove that it wasn't true," Trish said.

"Actually, I think the number was closer to two dozen," I corrected her.

"I'm going to keep telling it with my number," Trish explained. "It sounds better that way. It sounds as though Grace, Paige, and Emma got the ball rolling. Did they actually eat donuts in front of everyone?"

"They did, and I joined them, too," I said.

Trish looked around. "Where is Grace, by the way? You two are usually joined at the hip when something's going on in April Springs."

"She's handling some personal business," I said vaguely.

Trish knew me too well to just accept that. "Suzanne, are you okay?"

"I've been better," I admitted.

"Do you want to talk about it?" the diner owner asked me. "We can duck into the kitchen, where nobody will interrupt us. Well, nobody but Hilda."

Hilda Fremont was the main cook at the Boxcar Grill and also a friend of mine. "Thanks, but I can't just shove my head in the sand and hope this all goes away."

"Who said anything about sand? I was talking about two friends chatting and catching up," Trish answered.

I was about to decline again politely when my stepfather waved me over to his table. I looked at Trish and shrugged. "It looks as though I already have lunch plans, but thanks for the offer."

"That's fine, but just remember, I'm here if you need me," she said.

"I'm counting on it."

"So, burger and fries?" Trish asked me.

"What's the special?"

Lowering her voice and looking around before speaking, she told me softly, "You don't want to know. Trust me."

"How bad is it?"

"Hilda thinks it's amazing. Other people don't agree, but I promised her she could try it. Wow, that turned out to be a big mistake. I've been losing money hand over fist giving folks refunds, but this should get some of Hilda's crazier ideas out of her system."

"But you're taking a financial hit to do it," I pointed out.

"It's not that much, and I doubt I'll lose any customers. After all, where else are they going to have lunch in a town our size?"

I shook my head. "As opposed to donuts, which are sold in grocery stores, convenience stores, and even gas stations."

"Not Donut Heart donuts, though," she corrected me.

"That's true. Thanks."

"For keeping you away from a goulash that needs to be buried in the backyard or reminding you that you're an A-One donutmaker?" she asked me with a grin. "You're welcome either way."

"Let's just say it's for being my friend," I said as I gave her a quick hug.

"Right back at you," she said. "Now go before Phillip has a stroke."

I nodded and joined my stepfather. "Take it easy. I saw you."

"You didn't acknowledge it," he answered, clearly a little hurt by my behavior.

"Sorry. I've got some things on my mind. I'm having the mother of all bad days."

"So I've heard. Have you ordered yet?"

"I just did," I said as I surveyed his plate, nearly picked clean. "Did you actually try the day's special?"

"It wasn't half bad," he answered with a shrug. "Trish tried to talk me out of it, but I was hungry enough to eat the side of a barn, so I told her to bring me whatever she had that was hot and ready to eat."

"If you're finished eating, then why are you still here?" I asked him.

"I'm getting dessert," he said proudly.

"With Momma's skills, how can you even *look* at someone else's baked goods?" I asked him as Trish brought me my sweet tea and a small plate for Phillip.

"*She* doesn't make custard tarts," he said gleefully as Trish set it in front of him.

"I didn't even realize you liked them," I told him.

"I didn't, at least not before I started watching some British show on PBS with your mother. The man in the series loves custard tarts, so I decided to try one myself. He's right; they are amazing!"

"I'll take your word for it," I told him. I noticed he wasn't eating yet, so I added, "You don't have to wait on me."

"I'm not," Phillip said as his stomach gurgled a bit. "Maybe I ate my lunch a bit too quickly."

"Or maybe it's the goulash," I countered.

"No, it's me," he said. "I'll drink a little more sweet tea, and it will settle right down. So, who do you think tried to kill Harper Wilcox?" he added softly.

"We don't even know for sure that it was intentional," I answered in kind.

"Come on, what are the chances he'd eat something on his wedding day that put him in intensive care?" Phillip asked me. "You're too good an investigator to believe in coincidences."

"I appreciate the compliment, but sometimes coincidences do happen."

"Maybe, but I don't like it. At least it wasn't a donut that nearly killed him," Phillip said with a shrug.

"What? How do you know that? Have you heard something I haven't?"

"Evidently it was in the soda he drank," Phillip answered off the cuff. "There's something a bit odd about that, though."

"What's that?" I asked.

"From what I heard, Harper usually doesn't drink soft drinks, but he and Gabby both had one right after the ceremony."

Chapter 7

"WHY DID HE DO THAT?" I asked loudly enough for the entire diner to hear.

"Keep your voice down, Suzanne," Phillip said. "The chief is sitting on that information for now."

"Then how did *you* find out?" I asked him in a much softer voice.

"Professional courtesy, I suppose, which was why I told you. Don't spread it around, okay? I shouldn't have told you, and if Chief Grant finds out that I did, he's going to stop telling me things."

"My lips are sealed," I told him as Trish approached with my burger and fries.

"Even from Jake?" he asked me.

"Even what from Jake?" Trish asked as she approached with my food.

"He wants to know if I can keep a secret," I told her.

"Suzanne, you should know that *I* trust you, if that counts for anything," the diner owner said with a smile.

"That means a lot to me," I told her.

"Yeah, well, you've got plenty of flaws, but being a blabbermouth isn't one of them."

"Wow, I can feel the warmth of your love from all the way over here," I said with a grin.

"You should," she said.

"Trish, I need a word with you," Judge Hurley said gravely.

"I warned you," she told him, "but you wouldn't listen, so don't come crying to me."

"Point taken," he replied unhappily.

"Want a burger to go, on the house?" she asked him with a smile.

"I'll pay for it, but yes, that would be wonderful."

"Tell you what. I'll let you have it half off. Think of it as today's real special," she told him.

I hadn't seen Hilda behind her until I heard her voice. "Judge, what was wrong with the goulash you ordered?"

He looked more uncomfortable than I'd ever seen him before. "Hilda, the truth of the matter is that you can do better," the man answered bravely.

She looked a bit upset by his criticism, but then she turned to Phillip. "What about you?"

"I'm sorry, but I have to agree with the judge," my stepfather said calmly, showing his bravery more than when he'd gone after armed criminals in the past.

I half expected Hilda to explode, but instead, she looked at Trish and said softly, "You were right. I was wrong. Sorry, boss."

"It's okay," Trish said, taking her cook's arm in hers as they walked back toward the kitchen. "Hey, even Suzanne makes a donkey donut every now and then."

"I heard that," I told her loudly.

"You were meant to," she said with a laugh. I didn't even mind, because apparently it was exactly what was needed to defuse the tense situation. "Come on, Hilda. Let's chuck what's left in the trash together. It'll be fun."

"I'm not sure you know what that word really means," Hilda told her, but she was in good spirits, so who was Trish to argue about it?

Once they were gone, I turned back to Phillip and said softly, "Now let's get back to what we were talking about before. Do you think there's a possibility that someone was trying to kill *Gabby* and not *Harper* with that poisoned drink?"

"They don't know that, and I never claimed that it was true, either," Phillip corrected me. "Who's to say who that tainted drink was really meant for? It wasn't as though the cups were marked with their names on them, from what I heard."

"It seems kind of reckless though, doesn't it? *Anyone* could have grabbed that drink."

"It could have just as easily been a donut," Phillip reminded me.

"Is it wrong for me to say that I'm glad that it wasn't?"

"No, it only makes you human," he replied. "Is Jake going to help you dig into it?"

"Slow down," I told him. "Who said I was doing anything of the sort? Like you said, it wasn't my donut, so it's not my problem."

Phillip laughed at me. "Are you actually trying to tell me that somebody might have tried to poison your friend, managed to get her groom, all on the day of their wedding, and you're *not* going to investigate? Come on, Suzanne, tell that to someone who was born yesterday."

"Okay," I admitted. "I may dig into it a bit, but unless Gabby asks me to investigate, I'm going to try to keep my nose out of it."

"What's wrong? Are you losing your taste for it?" he asked me gently as I took a bite of my burger. "There's no shame in it if it's true. It happens to the best of us."

"Is that what happened to you?" I asked him, since we were being so open and candid with each other.

"That was part of it, but mostly, it was because of your mother. Before we got together I didn't much care about what happened to me, but after we found each other, life became a tad more important to me than it was before." For a man who wasn't particularly sappy by nature, it was quite the declaration of love for my mother.

"You're a good man, Phillip Martin," I said as I patted his hand. "I know that I don't say that very often, but it's important to me that you know I feel that way."

"You're not so bad yourself," he replied, clearly a bit uncomfortable by my public declaration. Shaking his head slightly, he added, "If your long list of cohorts become unavailable for some reason, I'd like to officially volunteer my services, not that there's much chance of that happening."

"Don't be so sure about that," I told him, and then I took another bite so I wouldn't have to talk about it anymore.

Ha. As though that was really an option.

"Something else is clearly bugging you. Is there trouble in Paradise?" he asked.

I decided it might do me some good to unburden myself. "Jake is upset with me for pushing him about him helping Stephen with the state police, Grace thinks I played some part in the entire scheme and I didn't tell her, which is just absurd, and Paige thinks I blame her for spreading the rumor that one of my donuts poisoned Harper Wilcox. Because of those things, every last one of them is avoiding me like the plague right now."

"Wow, you weren't kidding about having a bad day, were you?" he asked kindly as he touched my hand lightly.

"No, sir, not one bit."

"Then I'm here for you if you need me. All you have to do is ask." His phone rang, and he glanced at it and told me, "It's your mother." Into the phone he said, "Yes. No. Fine. Okay. Bye."

"Wow, that was a tough one to decipher," I told him. "What's up with Momma?"

"She's got to track down some woman named Bethany Halstead. Do you know anything about that?"

"Evidently, Bethany was rude to Geneva while she was trying to do some business for Momma," I started to explain.

"I wouldn't want to be in Bethany's shoes if that's the case," Phillip said with raised eyebrows. "Now I've got to go run an errand for your mother, but I'm here if you need me."

"Here?" I asked as I looked around the Boxcar Grill and smiled.

"Well, not here. But here," he added, waving his arms around. "I mean in general."

I saluted him and smiled. "Thank you, General," I said. "I don't know how you managed to do it, but you got me to smile on a day that has been particularly short of them."

"You're most welcome," he said, and then he headed for the front to settle his bill.

I hadn't been happy about it at the time when he and my mother had gotten together, but it had been good for her, and for me as well, if I was being honest about it.

When I reached the front to pay my own bill, someone was making a fuss with Trish, and I almost ignored it until I realized that it was the man who'd shouted to the crowd that my donuts were filled with poison.

Fate had sent him back into my path, so I decided to exact a bit of revenge for nearly ruining my business by one stray remark.

"I can't believe you had the nerve to stick around April Springs after that little show of yours earlier today," I snapped at him.

It took him a second to realize that I was the donutmaker he'd accused of handing out poisoned donuts earlier. "Lady, I didn't mean anything by it."

"That's not how it sounded to me," I said as Trish listened intently to our conversation.

"Is this guy bothering you, Suzanne?" she asked me.

The stranger said, "Listen, I just want to pay my bill and get out of here."

"Not so fast," I said, cutting his exit off. Several folks in the diner were watching us now, but I didn't care. This man needed to be punished for his thoughtless remark. It didn't help matters that I'd had a bad day so far, and he was going to get some of the brunt of it.

"You can't stop me from leaving!" he argued.

Trish walked past him with a meat cleaver in her hand and blocked the front door. "Really? Nobody's trying to stop you. You're free to leave once you pay your bill."

He scrambled for his wallet, jerking it out of his back pocket and ripping his pants as he did so. "All I have is a twenty."

"That'll work," Trish said. "Hilda? Could you come up here and bring your little friend?"

The cook came up almost instantly, carrying a knife that dwarfed the one in Trish's hand. "What's wrong, boss?" It must have been a new code phrase that they'd worked out for emergencies.

"This man is refusing to pay," Trish said calmly. "We're not going to let him leave until he does, are we?"

"I'm paying! I'm paying!" he shouted as he threw the bill at Hilda. "Keep the change! I'm getting out of here, and nobody better try to stop me."

At that moment, Officer Darby Jones came into the diner. When he saw the tableau playing out in front of him, he frowned before speaking. "What's going on here?"

"They're kidnapping me," he screeched. "Arrest them. Arrest them all!"

Darby shook his head. "I'm sorry. Were you under the impression that I was talking to *you*?" He looked at Trish. "What's going on?"

"He was giving me some trouble about paying, so I decided to try to convince him it was in his best interests to come across with the cash he owed me."

"That's a lie! I tried to pay!" the man protested.

Trish shrugged. "I suppose it's possible there was a misunderstanding about his bill, but there's something else you should know, Darby. This is the guy who told all of April Springs that Suzanne's donuts were poisoned."

Darby frowned again as he reached for his handcuffs.

The man shouted with glee, "You're all going to jail now! See how you like that!"

"What's your name?" Darby asked him cordially.

"Gary Block," he said. "Why do you need to know that? Is it for the arrest report?"

"It surely is," Darby said as he took the cuffs and used them on the protesting man.

"What? You're arresting *me*? Why? What did I do?"

"Disturbing the peace, for starters," Darby said as he started reading the man his rights.

"But *they* started *it*," he screeched. "She pulled a knife on me!" he said as he pointed at Trish. "They both did."

"They were just trying to get you to pay your bill," Darby said. "You were the one who shouted that Suzanne's donuts were poisoned. Buddy, you can't yell 'fire' in a crowded theater, and you can't yell out that somebody's donuts are poisoned when half the town's already had one."

"What is *wrong* with you people?" Gary Block whimpered as Darby motioned for me to open the door of the diner. I did as I was instructed and followed them outside, but not before turning to Trish and Hilda and thanking them. The entire diner started applauding, and the ladies both took bows before they returned to their stations.

I walked out with Darby and Gary Block. "Are you really going to arrest him?"

"Please don't do it," Gary pled. "I can't go back to jail."

"Why did you do it?" I asked him.

The handcuffed man frowned a moment before he spoke. "Forget it. It's not worth it. Some dude paid me a hundred bucks to do it. I'm not going to jail for him, though."

"Hang on a second," I told Darby, and then I looked hard at the handcuffed man. "Is that really the truth?"

"I still have the hundred in my shirt pocket," he said as he gestured with his shoulder. "Check and see. I'm not lying, lady."

"May I?" I asked Darby.

"Let me," he said, taking out a plastic evidence bag and reaching into Gary Block's shirt pocket. Sure enough, there was a hundred-dollar bill in his hand when he pulled it back out.

"Hey, I earned that fair and square," Block protested. "You can't keep it."

"Cool your jets," Darby said. "It might be evidence for the trial."

"Trial? For saying something innocent like that?" the man asked in stark disbelief.

"The charge is attempted murder," Darby explained to him.

"I didn't try to kill anybody!" the man said, nearly falling down the steps as he said it.

"Maybe not, but whoever poisoned Harper Wilcox was probably the same person who paid you to divert suspicion away from him, and that makes you an accomplice," Darby explained. "Come on. I need to interview you at the station."

As Darby started to lead him away, I touched the police officer's shoulder lightly. "Darby, I don't want to press charges. He's been punished enough for what he did to me."

"That's kind of you, Suzanne, but this goes beyond that now."

"How's Harper doing?" I asked.

"No news so far, at least none that I know about." He gave Block a gentle nudge. "Come on, sport, let's go."

"Where's your cop car?" the handcuffed man asked as he searched the parking lot for Darby's cruiser.

"It's such a pretty day, let's walk to the police station," Darby said. "It's just over there."

"I hate small towns!" Block snapped out.

"Well, don't rush to any judgments. We're pretty nice once you get to know us," I said.

He stopped walking for a second and then looked at me. I wasn't sure what he was going to say, but I was willing to bet that it wasn't going to be pleasant.

I was wrong, though.

"Ma'am, I'm sorry for what I did to you. I should have known better, but my greed got the better of me. I didn't think it would hurt anybody, but I can see now that I was wrong."

"Tell you what. Once you're out, come by the donut shop some morning, and I'll treat you to a donut and a cup of coffee."

"Thanks," he said, shaking his head.

"Come on, Mr. Block. The sooner we get you there, the sooner you can leave."

"You're really going to just let me go after you interview me?" he asked hopefully.

"Not right away, but I imagine you'll be out by the time Suzanne opens up in the morning, as long as you tell us the truth."

"Officer, my life of crime is officially over right now. I'll tell you whatever you want to know, and that's a promise."

Darby nodded as he winked at me. "I'm glad for you." He turned to me and added, "See you later, Suzanne."

"See you, Darby," I said as I watched them walk across the parking lot toward the police station together. It wasn't more than a hundred yards away, so they weren't in for that much of a stroll, but clearly, Gary Block didn't know that.

As I walked back toward my cottage, I realized that I'd left the diner without paying my bill!

At least I figured Trish and Hilda would give me the benefit of the doubt and not try to collect with their cutlery.

After I settled up my bill with Trish, who initially hadn't wanted to take my money, I walked the short distance to the cottage I shared with Jake. I hated that things were tense between us, and as soon as humanly possible, I was going to make things right with him. Not only was he my dear husband, but he was also one of my best friends as well. Grace was another one, and I hated the idea that both of them were unhappy with me, and that didn't even cover the fact that Paige couldn't bear being in the same room with me. If most folks in April Springs had a problem with me, I could find a way to live with it. In fact, they could bark at the moon for all I cared, but I didn't want my inner circle upset with me.

That was why I was surprised and happy to find Jake already back at the cottage when I walked through the door. After I made things right with him, I'd walk down Springs Drive and speak with Grace.

But one look at Jake's face told me that our petty squabble wasn't even on his radar at the moment.

Something had clearly happened, and I felt my stomach drop as I wondered just how bad the news he had to share was going to be.

Chapter 8

"DID SOMETHING HAPPEN? Is Harper dead?" I asked him, holding my breath as I waited for his answer.

"I have no idea," he answered.

"Then why are you so glum?" I asked.

"I don't like the way we left things earlier," Jake admitted. "Suzanne, you can't just push me when I say no to something."

"But what if I really *want* new drapes in the cottage?" I asked him, hoping to tease him out of his bad mood.

"This isn't about drapes, and you know it."

"I was trying to break the tension," I explained. "Evidently I did it badly." Before he could reply, I quickly added, "Jake, I was wrong. I'm sorry. I would love to promise you that it won't happen again, but we both know I can't do that. All I can say is that I'll try. Forgive me?"

I leaned into him for a kiss, but he took a step back. "This is serious, Suzanne. I can't do what I need to do if I'm worried about you pressing me on things I'm not allowed to share with you. I know most marriages shouldn't have secrets, but these aren't my stories to tell."

I nodded. "I get it. I said I was sorry."

"I just want to be sure you understand," he replied, easing up a bit.

"I do," I said.

"Good," Jake replied, the cloud leaving his expression. "Now how about that kiss?"

"I thought you'd never ask," I said. After a full minute, I pulled away. "I'm glad we got that settled. Now I have to go."

"Wow, that was quick," he answered. "Why rush off?"

"I need to make things right with Grace, too," I told him.

"Try saying what you said to me," Jake replied with a grin.

"I can't do that. I really didn't do anything wrong with Grace, so it's going to make things harder to fix."

"What are you going to do?" he asked.

"I don't know. I guess I'll find out the second I do it." I kissed him again quickly before I added, "You're not going anywhere soon, are you?"

"I really should get back to Chief Grant," he admitted.

"Then go, with my blessing. I won't even ask you what you're up to. How's that for turning over a new leaf? Shoot, I may even find an entire branch to turn over while I'm at it."

"A single leaf is fine with me. Would you like me to drop you off at Grace's on my way?"

"Thanks, but I need the steps to come up with a plan."

"Maybe you should circle around a time or two while you're at it," Jake replied.

"You think you're kidding, but I might have to. Stay out of trouble, okay?"

"I'm as inclined to take that advice as you are," my husband answered with a slight smile.

"That's a fair point. I'll see you for dinner."

"If I can get free," he warned me.

"Right back at you, then. Let's just say that I'll see you when I see you."

"And not a moment before," he added as he left the cottage. Jake's mood had dramatically improved since we'd made up, and honestly, so had mine.

One down, two to go. Paige would have to wait, though.

Grace had my full attention at the moment.

The only problem was that Grace wasn't home when I got there.

Could she have gone back to work, even though it was late afternoon, or had she simply taken off to cool down? I understood why she was upset with Stephen and maybe even Jake. I knew that I was just collateral damage, and I hoped that she'd see that I'd been innocent in all of this. Maybe a little time was what she needed.

Since I had some time on my hands and The Last Page was so close, I decided to walk the rest of the way down Springs Drive and speak with Paige. I wasn't sure I'd be able to do any good, but it was worth a shot. Besides, I had some new information that might just ease her conscience a bit.

"Suzanne, I'm not ready to speak with you yet," Paige said when I walked into her bookstore. It was always such a warm and welcoming place that it felt odd being ostracized from it.

"You don't have to say a word. Just listen."

"There's nothing you can say that's going to make me feel better," Paige replied, and a few of her customers started watching us.

I decided to ignore them. After all, it wouldn't be the worst thing in the world to happen if they overheard what I was about to tell Paige and even spread it around April Springs. After all, why shouldn't gossip help me for a change of pace and not hurt me?

"The man who lied about my donuts being poisoned was paid to do it," I told her loudly. "He would have said it whether you mentioned it or not. He was just waiting for the right moment, and when he saw it, he took it."

Paige looked confused. "Why would someone lie about your donuts, Suzanne, let alone pay someone else to do it?"

"My suspicion is that whoever really poisoned Harper Wilcox wanted to use my donuts as a distraction from the truth." I made sure to say that last bit as loudly as I could, knowing that the story would be spreading around all of April Springs before I even managed to leave the store.

"So then it *wasn't* my fault?" Paige asked, the hope clearly showing in her expression.

"It was not," I told her. "Are we good now?"

"If what you just told me is true, we certainly are," Paige answered.

"Would I lie to you?" I asked her with a grin.

"If you thought it would help me, I don't doubt for one second that you would," she answered honestly.

"That's fair, but I just happen to be telling you the truth."

"So, who paid that awful man to spread that story?" Paige asked.

"That's what the police are trying to find out even as we speak," I told her.

"Well, I'd be lying if I didn't say that hearing that is a relief. I hated the thought of causing you so much pain."

"No pain here," I told her, and then I hugged her.

After a few moments she pulled away. "Thanks, Suzanne."

"No need to thank me," I answered. "It's all part of the platinum deluxe friendship package."

"I didn't even realized I'd signed up for that one," the bookstore owner answered with a smile of her own.

"You opted for the basic package when you moved to April Springs, but I decided to give you a free upgrade. I hope you don't mind."

"Mind? I won't settle for anything else now that I know it exists," she answered.

"Excellent. Well, if you'll excuse me, I need to run back to the cottage and take a shower. I still reek of donuts even though I've already had one shower today."

"There are worse ways to smell," she allowed.

"True, but I get tired of it sometimes. I'll see you later, okay?"

"You can count on it."

The second shower back home felt great, and so did putting on new clothes, my kind of clothes this time instead of the fancy dress I'd still been wearing from the wedding. I didn't mind getting myself all gussied up, but what I really loved was wearing blue jeans and T-shirts, with jackets thrown in when the cold weather visited us in the foothills of the Blue Ridge Mountains. The air was beginning to chill at night, and I knew that slowly but surely, autumn and then winter would be upon us once again. I had a friend who'd moved to Sarasota, Florida, upon graduating from college. She claimed to love the constant warmth down there, but I lived for the changing seasons. It was worth the occasional snowstorm, ice storm, or even power outage in order to get that. Of course, that was easy for me to say when the weather was just starting to turn from the heat of summer to the chill of autumn. I might give a different answer in January or February, but for now, I was happy enough with the weather I had.

Now if I could only come up with who had tried to kill Harper Wilcox or Gabby Williams. I had a hunch that if I could figure that out, I'd discover who had slandered my donuts as well. I wasn't equating the acts of poisoning with rumormongering, but they were both crimes, at least in my mind.

I was just about to figure out what my next step needed to be when the doorbell rang.

Who could be visiting me at the cottage now? Since there was a potential killer on the loose in April Springs, I decided to get my trusty softball bat from the closet before I answered the door. It wouldn't stop a bullet, but then again, I didn't have any of Jake's old riot gear that might. Anything short of that, though, I was pretty sure I could handle. I wasn't afraid of another blunt instrument with the bat in my hands or even a knife.

After all, I had the reach.

After I peeked through the spyhole of the door, though, I knew I wouldn't be needing my bat after all.

It was a friend, and not a foe, who had decided to pay me a visit.

"Grace, I've been looking all over the place for you," I said as I tossed the bat on the couch.

"Why, were you going to try to beat some sense into me with that?" she asked with a soft smile as she watched the bat bounce twice and then land on the floor with a loud clang. I liked the aluminum over wood because of the way it felt in my hands, but it could be loud when it fell.

"Never," I said.

"Really?"

"I know how thick that skull of yours is. I'd have to use something much heavier than a softball bat to get through it." It was a risky thing to say, but I knew her well enough to realize that it was exactly what was called for at the moment.

"Fair enough. Listen, I'm sorry."

"I said the same thing to Jake earlier," I admitted. "Is the town putting something in our water supply besides fluoride?"

Grace frowned for a moment. "Let's get one thing straight. This apology is for you and only you. Do you understand?"

"I take it that you're still peeved at the men in our lives?" I asked her.

"That would be affirmative," she replied. "If it's all the same to you, I'd like to keep that separate between the two of us. I had no right to unload on you, and for that, I'm sorry. Can you accept that as it stands?"

"I can, and I will," I told her, and then I hugged her. I wasn't crazy about her still being so unhappy with my husband, but rationally, I knew that she felt as though she had legitimate reason to feel the way she did. I was going to have to butt out and let the two of them work it out for themselves, as much as that went against my basic nature.

"That's good. It's been killing me fighting with you," she said.

"I know just how you feel. In the last half hour, I've made up with Jake, Paige, and now you. I'm an emotional wet rag at the moment, but now I know that I at least have a shot at sleeping tonight."

"How did you bring Paige around?" she asked.

"The guy who shouted that my donuts were poisoned confessed to being paid by someone to do it. At the moment, Darby Jones is trying to find out who financed it."

"Wow, so they were using your donuts as a screen to protect them from what they really used. Man, that's dirty."

"I think so too," I said.

Just then, my cell phone rang.

I was about to ignore it when I saw who was calling me.

"It's Gabby," I said. "I've got to take this."

"I understand completely. Go on, answer it," Grace said, and I answered the call, hoping against hope that she wasn't about to share some tragic news with me about her new husband.

Chapter 9

"GABBY, WHAT'S GOING on?" I asked her, hoping beyond hope that it wasn't going to be tragic news from her.

"Suzanne, I need you at the hospital right now!" she said. "They are calling me back. Come now. Hurry!"

Before I could get another word out of her, she hung up on me.

"What was that all about?" Grace asked me as I grabbed my car keys.

"I have no idea," I admitted. "She wants me there with her. Come on."

Grace hesitated. "Did she ask for me, too?"

"No," I admitted. "But that doesn't mean she wouldn't want to see you."

"Suzanne, go see what she wants. She thinks the world of you. I don't want to butt into whatever she wants to discuss with you."

"I'm going, Grace. I don't have time to stand here and argue with you," I said as I hurried out the front door of the cottage toward my Jeep.

"I'll be at the house if there's anything I can do to help," she told me as she left my place right behind me. "I locked up. Go."

"I'll call you if I hear anything," I told her. "I'm sorry I have to run, Grace, but she needs me."

"You'd do the same thing if it were me asking you to come," she said. "Just don't wreck on the way to the hospital. We don't need any more excitement, do you understand?"

"I'll try not to. See you later," I told her as I got in and started my Jeep.

I had to ask a volunteer at the desk if Harper Wilcox was still in ICU, hoping that at least he was still among the living. "He's there, dear, but I'm afraid they are restricting his visitors to family only."

"I don't need to see him. I'm here for his wife," I told her as I rushed toward the intensive care unit.

Gabby was dabbing at her eyes when I walked into the ICU waiting area. I never would have made it that far if my friend, Penny Parsons, hadn't been nearby and escorted me back.

"Are you okay?" I asked Gabby as I slid onto the chair beside her. She was all alone, and I felt like a heel for not coming before she'd called me. I prided myself on being a good friend, but I wasn't feeling like one at all at the moment. "Is it Harper? Is he...." I couldn't even bring myself to ask the question.

"What? No, his condition hasn't changed. He looks so weak with those tubes hooked up to him and all of that machinery around him. Suzanne, I need you to do something for me."

"Can I go by your place and get you a change of clothes?" I asked her.

"What's wrong with what I'm wearing?" she retorted.

"Nothing. You look amazing. I just thought you might be more comfortable in something a little less...formal."

"Clothes don't matter at the moment," she said. It was an odd thing to hear a woman say who owned and operated an upscale clothing store, even if the items for sale were all gently used. She looked around down the hallway gauntlet Penny had just escorted me through. "Where's Grace?"

"Did you need her, too?" I asked her. Why hadn't she come with me when I'd asked her to join me? "I can have her here in ten minutes, fifteen tops," I told her.

"Do so, please. I have something I need from *both* of you."

At that point, a pretty young brunette nurse from the ICU area came out. She wore a nametag that said *Stephanie* on it, and she had a concerned expression on her face as she asked, "Ms. Williams? Are one of you ladies Ms. Williams?"

"I'm Mrs. Wilcox," Gabby corrected her.

"I'm so sorry. They told me to ask for a Ms. Williams." She looked honestly confused by Gabby's denial of her name. "Are *you* Mrs. Williams?" she asked me. "I'm new here. This is my first shift at the hospital."

"I'm the one who's sorry, child," Gabby said. "*I'm* Ms. Williams, or at least I was up until a few hours ago, when I became Mrs. Wilcox," she explained.

"Okay, I understand now," the girl said. "If you'd like, you can come back in for a few minutes."

Gabby turned to me to say something, but I cut her off. "Go. When you come back, we'll be here. Both of us will be."

"Do you promise?"

"I do," I said, and I immediately regretted my choice of words yet again.

Gabby flinched a bit at the repeating of her recent vow, but then the young nurse tapped her shoulder. "I'm sorry, but it needs to be now, Mrs. Wilcox."

Gabby hurriedly followed Stephanie while I took out my phone. Then I saw the sign that forbade cell phone use in the area. I walked out to the main lobby, where I knew that I'd be safe making a call, and dialed Grace's number.

She picked up before it had a chance to finish the first ring. "Suzanne? Is he dead?"

"Not so far," I told her. "Gabby wants to see you."

"She wants to see *me*?" Grace asked. "She must be delirious if she'd rather have me there with her than you."

"I didn't say that she *just* wanted to see you," I corrected her. "She wants us both. Come on, Grace, you need to get here as soon as you can."

"I'm on my way. You'll be there when I get there, right?"

"Of course I will," I told her. "I'll wait for you by the front entrance."

Grace was as good as her word, and nine minutes later, she came rushing through the front door of the hospital.

"It took you long enough," I told her sarcastically.

"Really? I had a police escort, so I'm not exactly sure how I could have gotten here any sooner," she said as we both started walking toward the ICU area.

"I was kidding," I told her. "Did Stephen actually give you an escort?"

"No, but Rick Handler did," Grace admitted. "He's been trying to get back on my good side ever since what happened a few months ago when Darby was the acting police chief."

"Gotcha," I told her.

"What's going on with Gabby?" she asked me.

The stern nurse who'd earlier denied me entrance without Penny's escort was still at her station, but evidently, my friend had said something to her, because she pointedly looked the other way when Grace and I walked past her.

"I don't know. She's back with him right now," I said.

Gabby chose that moment to meet us ten steps from the ICU. "He's holding his own, at least for now," Gabby reported. "Good," she said when she saw Grace. "You're here."

"If there's anything I can do..." Grace started to say when she was interrupted.

"As a matter of fact, there is. I need you and Suzanne to figure out who did this to my husband."

"Gabby," I said quickly, "Stephen Grant and Jake are both on the case. They're doing everything in their power to find the culprit."

"You don't understand," Gabby said. "I need you two working as well. You see, the doctors here aren't sure what kind of poison was used on Harper, and without that, they can't figure out what antidote to give him. If you don't do it, he's going to die."

"Surely they have lab tests and all kinds of ways to determine what the poisoner used," I said. I wanted to help her, but I'd never been put on the clock like that before, and I wasn't sure Grace and I could do anything to help her so immediately.

"Tests take time," she explained. "I need this from you both. Are you saying that you're both *not* willing to help me?" Gabby asked pointedly.

"Of course we'll help you," I told her, with Grace echoing my words almost at the same time that I said them. "We'll do whatever we can."

"Then why are you standing around here?" Gabby snapped out. "Go!"

The last bit was said so loudly that it caught the attention of several folks nearby.

"We'll do our best," I said as Grace and I started back for the front door.

"I need something better than your best," Gabby said pointedly. "I won't be a widow on my wedding day. Do you understand me? I just won't!"

"We're on it," Grace replied.

Once we were outside in the open air again, I said, "I don't even know where to start, do you?"

"Let's get my car back to the house so we can take your Jeep wherever we need to go," Grace replied.

"And then what?" I asked.

"We'll burn that bridge when we come to it," Grace answered.

She jumped into her company car, and I made my way to my vehicle. As we drove back to her place, I had a few moments to think as we raced down the road that would soon turn into Springs Drive and thus lead us back home. Gabby had given us a tall order, but I wasn't going to let that stop me from doing my best to help her.

I just wished I knew how.

"Thanks for following me home," Grace said as she got into my Jeep.

"I had a tough time keeping up with you. You were flying!"

"Hey, I know we're on a deadline here," she told me as she buckled her seatbelt. "Have you been able to come up with a game plan?"

"I have," I admitted as I drove less than two hundred yards and parked in front of Donut Hearts.

"We could have walked that," Grace told me as she got out.

"I can always drive back to the cottage, and we can walk from there, if you'd prefer to do it that way."

"No, this is good. So, why are we here? Are we going to check the donuts that weren't eaten at the event?"

"No, I told your husband I would save them for him, so I don't feel right digging through them, not that I'd even know what I was looking for."

"Anything out of the ordinary, I'd say," Grace told me.

"We'll call that Plan B," I said.

"Wow, do we even have a Plan A, Suzanne?"

"We're going to do a little digging, but you might not like it," I told her.

"As long as you don't have me rooting around in other people's trash cans, I'll be fine," Grace said, and then she looked at my face. "That's what we're doing, isn't it?"

"On the plus side, I've got some gloves in the shop we can use," I told her as I unlocked the front door to Donut Hearts.

"Why do I let you talk me into doing these things?" she asked as I retrieved some of the food-grade plastic gloves I used at the shop and handed her a pair. Almost as an afterthought, I tucked half a dozen of the industrial-grade trash bags we used at the store as well into my back pocket, or at least enough of them to get them to stay where I wanted them.

"Because you're a good person who wants to help Gabby and her new husband?" I asked her as I then slipped on a pair of the gloves myself.

"No, that can't be it," she answered with a slight smile.

"You can lie to yourself all you want, but you can't lie to me," I told her as I led her back out front and locked the place up yet again.

"Where are we looking, and what exactly are we looking for?" she asked me.

"'Where' is any trash can between the soda stand and ReNEWed," I told her. "'What' is anything that looks as though it may have contained some poison earlier."

"Liquid or powder?" Grace asked me.

"It could be either one," I admitted.

"That could be daunting."

"At least we'll be doing it together," I told her.

"I suppose that's something," she admitted. "Well, let's start diving into other people's garbage."

We went through six refuse cans without spotting anything that looked as though it might have once held poison in it, and I decided then and there that I wouldn't be having dinner later that night. I wasn't a delicate flower by any means, but some of the things we moved from one trash bag to another were enough to turn me off food for a very long time. It didn't help matters that besides the general crowd discards, spanning from dirty diapers to trashed food to things I didn't even want to guess at, there were quite a few donuts tossed in the trash that had been untouched, or at least uneaten, anyway.

"This is pointless," Grace said as we closed up yet another bag.

"Maybe so, but it's the only idea I could come up with," I admitted. "Look on the bright side. There are only two more sets of cans to go."

"The ones behind ReNEWed, and what other ones?" she asked.

"Mine at Donut Hearts. After all, my building is right beside Gabby's, so it's not that big a stretch to figure that someone dumped the container there after using the poison inside."

As we made our way to the back of ReNEWed, Grace asked, "Speaking of which, what about the trash cans inside the shop?"

"I imagine the police have already confiscated those," I told her.

When we walked in back of the new building, I was in for a surprise.

The cans there were empty too.

"Did somebody beat us to them?" Grace asked me.

"It appears that the April Springs Police Department had the same idea we did," I told her.

"Not entirely. After all, there were a great many trash cans we checked that they clearly didn't."

"True," I said, "but we haven't found anything yet, have we?"

"I wouldn't say that," Grace replied. "We found any number of things, none of which I ever want to think about again."

"I meant pertaining to the poisoning," I corrected myself.

"I knew what you meant," she said. "Do we really need to check your cans too? All I want to do right now is go home and take a long, hot shower."

"Go right ahead," I told her. "I don't mind finishing up here."

She appeared to think about it for a moment before she answered, "No, if you're trash can diving, then so am I. Let's get to it."

As I checked the second of my four cans out back, I saw something that shouldn't have been there. The trash normally held thrown-out food that had been nibbled on, napkins, containers from the supplies we used making donuts, and things like that.

What was definitely out of place was an aspirin bottle.

"What is this doing here?" I asked as I pulled the bottle out of the old donut box someone had jammed it into. I was happy that I was at least wearing gloves, so if there were any fingerprints on it, they wouldn't be mine.

"Maybe somebody had a headache and used the last two tablets before chucking the bottle," Grace said.

"It's possible, but why try to hide the empty container in my trash can?" I asked. I gently popped the top off the bottle, and though it appeared to be empty inside, I could see some powder in the bottom.

Grace asked, "What's in there?"

"Some kind of powder," I said, putting the top carefully back on.

"It's probably just a bit of aspirin," she said.

"Maybe, but what if it's not? I've got to get this to the hospital."

I pulled off my gloves, and as I did so, I wrapped the bottle in the palm of one of them.

"Can I drive?" Grace asked eagerly.

"No, I want to be sure we get there in one piece," I answered. "You can hold this," I added as I shoved our prize into her hands.

"Fine, but I bet I could get us there quicker even driving your Jeep."

"There's no doubt about it in my mind," I replied, "but there's no way I'm handing you the keys. You know that, don't you?"

"Hey, it doesn't hurt to ask," Grace answered as we hurried for my vehicle parked in front of my shop.

As I rushed into the ICU, I said, "Gabby, we might have found something."

"It might be nothing though, so don't get your hopes up," Grace added.

Then I looked at the expression on Gabby's face.

"What happened, Gabby?" I asked her.

"He's fading fast, Suzanne," she said, and then she collapsed into my arms.

Penny came back when she saw what was happening. "Do you need any help?"

"We found something," I said. "Grace, give her the bottle."

She handed our friend the aspirin container.

"It was buried in my trash can," I explained. "Can you test it to see if it's poison?"

"I don't do that, but I know where to take it," she said as she took the bottle from Grace.

"Careful. There may be fingerprints on it," I cautioned her.

"I'll let them know in the lab," she answered as she took off.

"What can we do now, Gabby?" I asked her as I finally got her settled down a bit.

"Stay here and sit with me," she said.

"I'll go see if I can find us some coffee," Grace replied, wanting to give us some privacy, no doubt.

"If you don't mind, I'd like you here too," she told Grace. "Please?"

"Of course," Grace replied, and then we all sat together and waited, for what, we weren't exactly sure of just yet.

Chapter 10

"HOW'S HARPER'S BEST man, by the way?" I asked Gabby after a few minutes of all of us sitting there together in silence. "Is he still here?"

"He *is* a patient, but it's not as bad as they thought it might be," Gabby told me. "He's in a room in another wing, but he'll probably just have to stay a day or two for observation."

"What happened?" Grace asked.

"Harper's first choice for best man was in a car accident on his way to the wedding," I explained. I turned back to Gabby and asked, "What was his name again?"

"Emerson Glade," she said.

"How do he and Harper know each other?" I asked. I was mostly just trying to keep her mind off the fact that her new husband was struggling for his life a few feet away from us, but I was interested as well.

"Emerson and Harper own some mutual business ventures together," Gabby said a bit absently. "In fact, they were hoping to make a killing on a deal next week, but that's not going to happen now. I just pray they make it."

"Gabby, he's in good hands," I told her as I patted her shoulder.

She didn't draw back from it, and I wasn't a hundred percent sure that she'd even felt it. "They can only do so much, Suzanne."

"You've got to keep your hope alive," Grace told her from the other side.

"I'm trying," Gabby answered, "but it's not easy."

A doctor came out with absolutely no expression at all. As he approached us, Gabby reached for our hands, one on either side of her, to brace herself for the news to come.

I took a deep breath and prayed that I'd someday get the feeling back in the hand that Gabby was crushing, but I'd worry about that later.

At the moment, all I cared about was Gabby.

"I have news. I was right about the poison Mr. Wilcox ingested," the doctor said. I noticed the tag on his lab coat said, "Jeffords."

"Was it the same thing that was in the bottle we brought in, Doctor Jeffords?" I asked him.

He shrugged as if to dismiss my question. "It merely confirmed my earlier suspicions, but I was already in the process of beginning his treatment when we received verification from the sample," Jeffords said officiously.

"What was it?" Gabby asked him haltingly.

"Without getting too technical, the component in question is usually found only in certain industrial cleaners, so it took me some time to work it out."

"Is he going to be all right, then?" Gabby asked. I could feel her shaking under the strain of the day's events.

"Unfortunately, it is too soon to say. We're doing everything in our power at the moment, but the next twelve to twenty-four hours are critical," he said. The doctor didn't sound particularly hopeful to me. In fact, it seemed as though once he'd figured out what the poison was, he was rapidly losing interest in the case.

A nurse whispered something to him, and he said, "I've got to go. If you'll excuse me...."

Once he was gone, the nurse lingered and motioned me to one side.

When I joined her away from Gabby and Grace, she asked softly, "You're friends with Penny Parsons, aren't you? You're Suzanne Hart?"

"I am," I admitted. "Have we met?"

"I've only been here a few weeks, but there's something you should know."

"What's that?"

"*He*," she said as she gestured in the direction of the doctor who had just left, "had no clue what was wrong with Mr. Wilcox. Sure, he's going to write up the report to make himself out to be some kind of hero, but you're the ones who saved his life."

"I'm grateful to you for telling me, but should you have?" I asked her with a hint of a smile.

"No, absolutely not. That's why I didn't say a word to you just now," she answered, winking at me. "I just wanted to wish you a good day."

"To you as well," I said. "Thank you."

"Thank *you*," she answered. "I *hate* losing patients."

"I can't even imagine how you do what you do," I told her gratefully.

"Hey, don't sell yourself short. Penny's been telling me about your amazing donuts. I can't wait to try one myself."

"Come by any morning I'm working, and I'll give you anything your heart desires."

She laughed. "Anything? How about a faithful man, or a magic lamp with three wishes all ready for me? Shoot, I'd even take the numbers to the next winning lottery ticket."

"How about three donuts, your choice of flavor?" I asked her with a smile.

"Wow, that's almost as good as what I asked for," she answered. "By the way, I'm Colleen Dupree."

"It's nice to meet you, Colleen Dupree," I said.

"Anyway, I've got to get back. I just thought you should know. Could we keep it just between us, do you think?"

"I've already forgotten all about it," I told her with a small laugh.

"Penny was right. You are nice."

"Hey, spend your days around donuts and see if it doesn't happen to you, too."

"No, thank you. If I had your job, I'd weigh eight hundred pounds."

Taking in her petite frame, I countered, "I highly doubt that."

"That's because you've never seen me eat," she answered with a grin as she took off down the hallway.

"Who was that?" Grace asked me.

"A new friend, I believe," I told her.

"You do manage to collect the oddest assortment of people, don't you, Suzanne?" Gabby asked me pointedly.

"I like to think so. After all, I was lucky enough to collect both of you, wasn't I?"

Neither one of them had an answer for that, so we all settled back into amiable silence as we waited for more news.

"Hey, ladies. Any news on the patient?" Chief of Police Stephen Grant asked us twenty minutes later. I'd been trying to figure out how to break free of Gabby so Grace and I could get back to work, but every time I'd tried to bring it up, she'd cut me off.

"No news," Gabby told him. "Why are you here and not out trying to find out who poisoned my husband?" she added sharply.

"Ma'am, I've got everybody I can spare working on it, but crime hasn't stopped in April Springs. I've got to make sure *all* of our citizens are protected."

"Like you protected my husband?" she snapped.

"Gabby, I know you're upset, but that's no reason to take it out on the chief of police," I scolded her. "He's doing everything in his power to solve this case."

"I know he is," Gabby said as she slumped back in her chair again. "I'm sorry, Chief," she told him.

"No worries," Stephen said. "I was wondering if I might borrow my wife and Suzanne while I'm here."

"Go on," Gabby said reluctantly.

"Gabby, we need a chance to do what you asked us to do," I reminded her. I wasn't about to blatantly say it in front of the chief of police, but Grace and I had our own set of skills we could be using to help the investigation. Just because we found the source of the poison didn't mean that everything else was solved.

"Okay, you're right. Check in with me if there are any developments, will you?" she asked, almost pleading with us.

"You do the same," I said.

The chief stepped away, and Grace and I followed him back out front to the main lobby. I glanced back at Gabby before I left, and I saw a sad, broken woman. I hated to leave her, but honestly, what choice did I have?

"First of all, that was nice work finding the poison used," Stephen told us both once we were out of earshot of everyone else.

"Officially, it wasn't needed," I told him.

"Yeah, we heard that the report won't even mention what we did," Grace added.

"The official hospital report might read that way, but I'm going to put in mine that you two are the only reason Harper Wilcox has any chance at all."

"Doctor Jeffords still isn't sure it's going to matter," I reminded them. "We were almost too late to do Harper any good."

"Well, at least you did *something* productive, which is more than I can say at the moment." He turned to his wife and added, "Grace, could I have a minute?"

"It's not necessary," she said. "I know you're busy."

"I'm never too busy for you," he told her.

She patted his cheek and actually smiled at him. "We can have this conversation later. For now, all you have to do is figure out what really happened to Harper Wilcox."

"We know what happened," Stephen Grant said. "Somebody tried to kill him."

"Maybe, maybe not," I said softly.

"What? Do you want to tell me what's going on in that devious little mind of yours, Suzanne?" he asked me.

Before I could answer, Grace said, "I hate to be indelicate and all, but I've really got to go to the bathroom." She turned to her husband and said, "Stephen, I'll see you later."

"Does that mean that all is forgiven?" he asked her hopefully.

Her smile quickly faded as she said, "I said we'd discuss it later. What do you think?"

"I'd really rather not say," he admitted.

"That's maybe the smartest thing you've said to me in days," Grace said as she headed off down to the closest public restroom.

"Man, she's really upset, isn't she?" the police chief asked as he watched his wife leave.

"I refuse to answer on the grounds that I might incriminate my best friend."

"Yeah, I don't blame you," Stephen replied. "What did you mean by what you said earlier?"

"Don't try to act all innocent with me. I know you've already considered the possibility that Gabby was the intended target, not Harper."

"Where did you hear that?" the chief asked me pointedly.

"I protect my sources," I told him.

"You don't have the right to. When I find out who blabbed that to you, I'm hauling them in for obstruction of justice." Chief Grant was visibly upset. Uh-oh. I'd blown it by saying anything to him, but I wasn't going to compound the error by mentioning my stepfather by name.

"Hey, we're on the same side, remember?" I told him, trying to coax him out of his anger.

"I know, but I've got next to nothing, and to make matters worse, *you* found that poison, not me or my people."

"Hey, it was sheer dumb luck that we stumbled across it," I told him, trying to downplay what we'd done. "Who could have imagined that the container used would be dumped into my trash can at Donut Hearts."

"You and Grace, evidently," he said a bit glumly.

Officer Rick Handler came into the front, obviously looking for his boss. As he approached, he held back a bit.

I nodded in his direction. "It appears that one of your officers needs to speak with you."

He turned, and as soon as he saw who it was, he motioned Officer Handler to join us. "What do you need?" he asked him abruptly.

"It can wait," he said as he looked at me.

I got the message. "I'll give you two some privacy."

He nodded. "Thanks."

They were still talking when Grace came back and joined me, being careful to skirt around the two April Springs police officers. "I thought he'd be long gone by now," Grace told me softly.

"I blew it with him earlier," I confessed.

"What did you do? Suzanne Hart, if you're meddling in my marriage, I'm not going to be happy. Do you understand?"

"I wouldn't dream of it," I said. I considered bringing up Stephen's desire to join the state police with her again, but one glance at her expression told me that wouldn't be the wisest thing to do.

"Good decision," she said after watching the emotions change on my face.

"Which one?"

"Dropping it," she said.

"I'm sure I don't know what you're talking about," I told her with a slight smile.

"I'm sure you don't," she echoed, smiling a bit herself.

If the chief was in hot water with his wife, which he was, it was no business of mine. Certainly not if it put me in the soup with him.

"Okay, don't say I never share," Chief Grant told us as he rejoined us. Officer Handler was already gone, and I had to wonder if he had been assigned a new task as soon as he'd accomplished whatever he'd come to tell his boss. "It's about Emerson Glade."

"What about him?" I asked, clearly confused by this turn of events.

"He was supposed to be Harper's best man, but he got into a car accident on his way to the ceremony in April Springs."

"We already know that. What does that have to do with the price of eggs in Charlotte?" I asked him.

"Why would I care about the price of eggs in Charlotte?" Chief Grant asked, clearly confused by my segue.

"You shouldn't," I said. "I'll ask you one now. Why should we care about Emerson Glade's accident?"

"Because it's pretty clear that it was no accident, no matter what Emerson may think," he said softly. "We just got an eyewitness account of the wreck from someone who was driving two cars back. Evidently, someone deliberately tried to ram Glade's vehicle and drive it into a tree, not once but twice. Something's going on here, and I mean to get to the bottom of it."

Chapter 11

"DO YOU THINK THE WRECK had something to do with the poisoning?" I asked the police chief.

"It's the only way this mess makes sense, isn't it?" he asked me softly.

"So then you believe the poison was meant for Harper and not Gabby from the start," Grace added.

"I'm not even surprised that you knew about that, too," Chief Grant told his wife. "There's nothing the two of you don't talk about, is there?"

"Not much," we both said at the same time.

"Why would someone want to kill both men on the same day, though?" I asked.

"I've got some people looking into their business dealings," he said. "It feels like the most likely scenario right now, but we all know that can change by the minute."

"You'll figure it out," Grace told her husband. "I have faith in you."

"Do you? I've got to tell you, that's nice to hear. Listen, I know things are crazy right now, but if I could have a few minutes of your time, that would make my day go a whole lot better. To be honest with you, there hasn't been much right with it so far."

He looked as though he were about to break down, and I felt my heart go out to him, but it wasn't my decision.

Evidently Grace couldn't take it either. "Fine. I can give you a few minutes."

I patted my pockets. "Blast it all, I left my keys on the bench beside Gabby. I'll be right back."

"Sure you did," Stephen Grant said.

"Hey, we all make mistakes," I told him.

Grace mouthed the words "Thank you" to me, and I nodded in return.

That would give them a chance to chat, but it would also give me the opportunity to speak with Gabby again about her new husband. I hated to grill her when she was so vulnerable, but I was doing it at her request.

"I thought you left already," Gabby said as she looked up at me from her seat.

"I did," I told her as I sat back down beside her. "I just couldn't bear the thought of being so far away from you, so I came back." I said the last bit with a smile. I knew it was a gamble, but when it came to my relationship with Gabby, the entire thing was kind of a crapshoot.

She pursed her lips and then smiled at me. It was a sight well worth the risk I'd taken. "Ha ha. Why are you really here?"

"I wanted to give Grace and Stephen a few minutes of privacy," I admitted. "But I also wanted to speak with you about something. How well do you know Emerson Glade?"

"Harper's best man? We've had dinner a few times, with Harper of course. Why? Has he taken a turn for the worse? I nearly forgot about his accident."

"That's the thing. What if it wasn't an accident?" I asked her.

Gabby didn't take long to reach the same conclusion we all had earlier. "Do you honestly think they're related?"

"I don't know, but it makes me wonder," I said. "What's going on with these businesses they own together?"

"Harper doesn't talk about that part of his life with me," she said, her lips pursing together for a moment after she did.

"At *all*?" I asked. "That doesn't sound like something you'd be okay with."

"Of course I'm not," Gabby snapped. "Sorry, that shouldn't have been directed at you. Harper enjoys too many risks for my taste, and he tends to think that every flier he takes is going to work out. It's gotten him into trouble a few times in the past, but he always manages to dig himself out of it."

"What exactly are the two of them into right now? Do you know?"

"I don't, but I know someone who does. You need to speak with Deidra Lang."

"I don't believe I've ever heard of her," I admitted. "Where might we find her?"

"She's Emerson's secretary, and if you ask me, she's hoping to elevate her status to Mrs. Emerson Glade sometime very soon," Gabby said.

"Is there any chance of that happening? I mean before the accident?"

"I honestly have no idea," Gabby admitted.

"Where might I find her?" I asked her.

"You *might* find her in Union Square where Emerson has his office. Then again, she *might* be in Maple Hollow. I understand she loves antiquing. But where you *will* find her is over in the next wing of the hospital, where they're keeping an eye on Emerson. She came by earlier and told me that she's not leaving his side, and I believe her."

"Can you give me a description of her?" I asked Gabby.

"She's a little over six feet tall, has red hair down to her waist, and green eyes that any cat would envy. I suppose some men find her attractive, the ones who like the skinny, ethereal types, goodness knows why that might be."

"Thanks," I said. "I'll do a bit more poking since I'm already here."

"Be careful around Deidra," Gabby warned me.

"Careful in what way?" I asked, curious about what Gabby was implying.

"Suzanne, if she considers you a threat, she'll come after you," she said.

I had to laugh. "Gabby, I'm a happily married woman. There's no way I'm interested in her boss, and I'll be more than happy to tell her that."

"Just makes sure she believes you," Gabby said quietly.

"Gabby, did something happen between the two of you?" I asked, curious about my normally boisterous friend's reaction.

"Nothing I can prove," was all that Gabby would say. "Just heed my words."

"I will," I said. "So, there's nothing you can tell me about Harper's financial situation at all. Is that right?"

"It is," she said, and then she frowned again.

"Gabby, what are you not telling me?" I asked her.

"It's probably nothing," she replied. "Forget I said anything."

"Like that's going to happen. There may be only one person in April Springs more stubborn than you are, but you happen to be looking at her."

"I'm not sure I agree with your assessment," Gabby answered, and then smiled softly for a moment as she added, "Though I will admit that you're in the running. I'm sure it's nothing, and I don't want you to take this the wrong way, but something odd did happen yesterday."

"What was it?" I asked her, tensely waiting for her response.

"Harper brought an old friend of his by ReNEWed when I was getting ready for today's doubleheader."

"What's so odd about that?" I asked her.

"Nicholas Sutherland had some paperwork for me to sign. He's been Harper's insurance agent for years, and my husband-to-be wanted us to take out life insurance policies on each other, just in case."

The very idea of proposing such a thing on the eve of his wedding day chilled me for a moment. "Gabby, how much was the policy for?"

"One million dollars," Gabby said, her features slackening a bit as she said it. "Suzanne, do you think there's the slightest chance that my new husband had a premonition that someone was going to try to kill him on our wedding day?"

I wished that I had a more definitive answer for her, but at the moment, all I could say was "I honestly have no idea."

It was a tough way to leave her, but my time was up. I had to find Grace and then go speak with Deidra Lang.

When I got back out front, Chief Grant was already gone.

"How did *that* go?" I asked Grace as I joined her.

She just waved a hand in the air in response. "Nothing I care to get into right now. Let's get out of here, shall we?"

"Funny you should say that. There's someone here in the hospital we need to speak with before we go."

Grace frowned at me. "Harper is fighting for his life. I doubt they're going to let us just walk back there and start grilling him. As for his partner, from what I've heard, Emerson Glade is a bit better, but he's not receiving visitors either."

"There's someone else who might be though," I told her. "Gabby suggested we speak with Emerson's personal assistant. Apparently she's a tall, skinny redhead who is extremely territorial when it comes to her boss."

"She's not in love with him, is she?" Grace asked me as we started for Emerson's room.

"I suppose so. Gabby believes that she wants to marry him."

"Then let's go speak with her," Grace said.

I put a hand on her arm outside the room number we'd gotten. "Gabby told me we need to tread lightly with this woman. I don't know much about her, but clearly, Deidra Lang scares Gabby a little, so I'm not sure how much time I really want to spend pressing her."

Grace whistled softly. "*Gabby's* afraid of her? What kind of monster must she be?"

"I don't know, but we need to find out. Oh, there's one more thing."

"Wow, you certainly took advantage of my absence," Grace remarked.

"Hey, I was just trying to give you some privacy. Your poor husband looked as though he wanted to cry when I left."

She just shrugged. "He's better now, but before you ask, things are still tense between us. Now, what else did Gabby tell you?"

I was about to share that bit of new information about the insurance policies when the hospital room door opened and an attractive redhead popped her head out. "Would you two please find somewhere else to gossip? There is a very sick man in here."

It wasn't exactly the best way to meet Deidra Lang, but we didn't really have any choice at that point.

I put on my bravest smile as I stuck out my hand. "You must be Deidra. I've heard so much about you. How's Emerson doing, really?"

My aggressive friendly manner put her off stride, and it was clear she wasn't quite sure how to handle me. In the end, her Southern manners kicked in, and she took my hand, squeezing it for barely a second before releasing it again. "The doctors say there's nothing physically wrong with him, but he's still blanking out as to what happened to him this morning. That can't be a good sign, can it?"

I had no idea, but it wouldn't do me any good admitting it. "I would certainly think not. I'm guessing that we can't see him, but may we have a minute of *your* time?"

She glanced back inside. "I really shouldn't leave his side."

"I promise that it won't take long. We're trying to find out who ran him off the road, so anything you do to help us would be greatly appreciated," I said.

"We'll be sure that Emerson knows what a loyal employee you've been to him in his time of need," Grace added.

Deidra's expression grew grim for a moment, and I saw a flash of the temper Gabby had warned me about. How in the world could this delicate-looking woman produce such an intense expression of dislike so easily? "I am much more than a loyal employee," she said defiantly.

"Of course you are," I said, doing my best to smooth things over with her. "That's why we need your help. Deidra, who do you think might have tried to kill both of your bosses on the same day?"

"*Harper* isn't my boss," she corrected me acidly. "*Emerson* is," she added as she gestured back into the room.

"Forgive me. I misspoke. The two men have some business together, though, don't they, or did I hear that incorrectly as well?"

"No, you're not wrong about that," she admitted. "But I can't really discuss confidential matters with you." Deidra got a puzzled expression on her face as she asked, "Who exactly are you two, anyway, and why are you so concerned about Emerson?"

"We help the police out from time to time with their investigations," Grace said smoothly. "Gabby knows all about us, so she came to us and asked us for our help. In the course of our investigation, we learned that Emerson and Harper had some business dealings together and that they were good friends as well."

"Who told you that?" she asked me suspiciously.

"It's hardly a leap to figure that part out, given the fact that Emerson was going to be Harper's best man today," I explained.

"I'm curious about something," Grace asked. "If you two are as close as you claim to be, why weren't *you* in the car with Emerson when the accident occurred?"

That clearly struck a nerve with Deidra. "I was back at the office, taking care of some paperwork for him, and then I had a personal matter to attend to before the ceremony. I was coming later, but Emerson was insistent that everything be finalized this morning."

I took a wild shot in the dark. "It wasn't about the new insurance policy between the two men, by any chance, was it?"

The expression on her face told me that I'd scored a direct hit. "How did you know about that?"

"This isn't our first time investigating suspicious circumstances," Grace chimed in, though she was nearly as impressed by my revelation as Deidra had been.

"I'm guessing the policies were for one million dollars each. Am I right?"

"That is correct," she said.

"When did they become active?" Grace asked her, an excellent question. "Before or after Emerson's accident?"

"Definitely before, by about an hour," Deidra said, clearly unhappy about the conclusion she'd clearly just jumped to. "So his *partner* did this to him? I'm going to kill him myself if he's not already dead," she said fiercely as she tried to storm past us.

We blocked her from going after Gabby's new husband, but it wasn't easy. "We don't believe Harper had anything to do with what happened to Emerson," I told her. "You need to take a deep breath before you do something you'll regret."

"Think about how Emerson will react if you're wrong," Grace added. "It could taint your relationship forever."

That was the only thing that stopped her. My friend and investigative partner had found Deidra's weakness, and she had exploited it to the max. It had been a good lever to use, probably the only one that would do any good, and Grace had seized on it instantly.

Forget about Deidra being a threat.

I reminded myself not to get on *Grace's* bad side.

"Fine," Deidra said, slumping a little as a bit of the earlier fire went out of her. "But he'd better hope and pray that he had nothing to do with Emerson's accident, or he'll regret it for as long as he lives."

There was absolutely a threat there, but I decided to let it go, at least for the moment.

"Is there anyone you can think of who might want to see *both* men come to harm on the same day? It's just too big a coincidence for us to swallow, and it's also why we don't think Harper *or* Emerson had anything to do with each other's condition at the moment," I asked her once I was certain she was calm again.

"Actually, I can think of two people who might have wanted to harm them both," she replied.

"Would you care to share their names with us?" I pushed her a bit.

"I'd better not," Deidra replied, glancing back at her boss's bed. I couldn't actually see the man from where we were standing, but I could hear someone stirring inside. Was he eavesdropping on our conversation to see what he could learn?

"We're trying to help, remember?" Grace asked her softly.

"You just want to help Gabby Williams," she protested. Well, she wasn't entirely wrong, but if the two events were tied together, then we couldn't help but look out for her boss as well.

"We want to find who's behind everything that has happened today and make them pay for what they've done," I said solemnly.

"Fine, but if you tell anyone I said something to you, not only will I deny it so convincingly that you'll start to doubt you heard anything from me in the first place, but I'll make sure you are both punished for breaking my trust. Do we understand each other?"

"We do," I said, seeing a bit of that temper that seemed to constantly brew just below the surface in this woman.

"Very well. If I were you, I'd speak with Vance Wilkerson and Thomas Roberts."

"What do they have to do with what happened today?" Grace asked.

"Vance has always hated Harper, and he threatened to kill Emerson two days ago because of a supposed affair my employer is having with his wife. Thomas believed that the partnership between Harper and Emerson cost him close to a million dollars on a recent deal he lost out on at the last second. Right in front of my face, Thomas told them both that he wasn't going to take it lying down, and Vance said he'd ruin their lives *and* their construction ventures with all of his contacts, so maybe you should go talk to those two instead of pestering me."

Chapter 12

"YOU SEEM AWFULLY CLOSE to your boss," I said, refusing to take the hint that Deidra wanted us to leave.

"What if I am? What's your point?" she asked, the chip on her shoulder showing clearly.

"Why did Vance Wilkerson believe that Emerson was the reason his marriage broke up?" Grace asked her gently. "*Were* she and your boss having an affair?"

"That? It was nothing," Deidra said. "In fact, most of it was in Jenny's mind."

At that moment, a well-built blonde wearing a short skirt and a tight blouse, clutching a bouquet of flowers, turned the corner and started toward us. It was clear that she was there to see Emerson. The moment she spotted Deidra, she hissed, "What are *you* doing here? He *fired* you, remember?"

Deidra looked as though the other woman had slapped her face. "He didn't mean it, Jenny!"

"I heard him. Believe me. He meant it," Jenny Wilkerson answered with a snap in her voice. She turned her attention to Grace and me. "Beat it, ladies. He's mine."

"As honored and thrilled as we are to be mistaken for your competition," I told her, "we're both married."

"Big deal. So am I," Jenny said.

"Okay, then we love our husbands," I countered.

She just shrugged. "You've got me there." Jenny then turned back to Deidra. "What are *you* still doing here?"

"I'm Emerson's emergency contact," she said proudly. "I'm not going anywhere."

"Just because your name's on a form doesn't mean he's yours. That's paperwork, not love."

"Do you honestly think that he loves *you*?" Deidra asked her loudly. "If you do, then you're delusional."

"*I'm* delusional? You're nothing but a walking cliché. The secretary *never* ends up with her boss, no matter how many romantic comedies say otherwise."

"You can't see him!" Deidra snapped, and I saw more of the fire Gabby had warned me about. Wow, if Deidra was a force to be reckoned with, what must Jenny be if she managed to intimidate the bully?

"Try to stop me. I dare you."

As Jenny walked forward, Deidra knocked the flowers out of her hand and positioned herself in front of the closed door. "Bring it, witch."

"Should we do something?" I asked Grace as the two women started to face off.

"I know we don't have popcorn, but I still want to see the show," my best friend said. "I know Jenny looks tough, but I'll bet ten bucks on Deidra. Care to take that bet?"

"I'm not betting on either one of them," I said.

Grace was about to reply when a security guard came around the same corner Jenny had just traversed earlier. "What's going on here?"

"Beat it, buster," Jenny told him. "This is none of your business."

"The name's Macy, and you'd better believe that it's my business. You both need to leave."

"I'd love to see you try to make me," Jenny replied, taking her gaze off of Deidra for a second.

That turned out to be a mistake. Much to all of our surprise, Deidra launched herself at Jenny, knocking her to the floor and falling on top of her as she fell as well.

Macy shrugged and then got out his taser. "I warned you."

"Stop it," Jenny shouted as she tried to pull herself free. "You don't have to do that."

"If you both aren't on your feet and out of here by the count of ten, you're both getting zapped." Almost to himself, he said, "I finally get to use this thing. I can't wait to see how much it hurts."

That got their attention. The women pulled themselves apart and stood a few feet apart from each other, glaring the entire time.

"You wouldn't really have shot us with that thing, would you?" Jenny asked.

"It's my job," he said with a shrug, "so yeah, I would have. Leave right now. Both of you."

"I'm not going anywhere," Deidra said as she moved back in front of her boss's, or ex-boss's, room, depending on who you believed.

"Then you get the zap," he said a little too enthusiastically for my taste.

"Fine, I'll go," Deidra said, watching the weapon closely.

"*Both* of you," Macy said loudly.

They walked away, though clearly not together.

"What if they fight out in the parking lot?" I asked the security guard as I watched them go.

"Then it's Toby's problem," he said.

"Would you really have zapped them?" I asked him.

"Yes, ma'am. You'd better believe it."

"If they come back, can I do it?" Grace asked him with a grin.

"Do you honestly think I'm going to let *you* have all of the fun? I'm not going to have any trouble from you two, am I?"

"No, sir. Not one bit, sir," I answered.

"You don't have to call me sir."

"I do when you're eager to zap somebody with that thing," I corrected him.

He just chuckled. "Maybe that's a fair point. Carry on."

"You too, and don't zap anybody you don't have to," Grace told him.

"I'll try not to, but I'm not making any promises," Macy answered.

Now that we were alone, I did something I'd been wanting to do since we'd met Deidra. I walked over to the door and opened it slightly.

An older man was in bed, and if something was wrong with him, I couldn't tell it from where I stood.

And then a monitor started to beep.

A moment later, a crowd of doctors and nurses rushed into the room, kicking us out in the process.

They closed the door behind us, so we couldn't see what was going on.

"What should we do?" I asked Grace.

"I think we should hang around and see what happens," she said. "How about you?"

"I would like to know myself," I admitted.

We took up positions outside the door, and before long, the team came back out of the room, this time at a much slower pace.

"Is he dead?" I asked, having a hard time believing a man's life had just ended not twenty feet away from me.

"What? No. One of the monitors on the bed came unplugged," a nurse told us. "He's awake, and he's asking for somebody named Deidra. If that's one of you, then you should go on in."

What choice did we have? I didn't have to actually lie and say that either one of us was named Deidra, but if Emerson Glade was awake, I wanted to speak with him. "Thanks," I said, taking Grace's arm in mine as we walked into the hospital room.

"Who are you two? How bad did I hit my head, anyway? Am I married to one of you?" Emerson Glade asked as he moved his bed into a more upright position.

"You should be so lucky," Grace told him. "We're friends of Gabby Williams."

"We are?" I asked her with a smile.

"We're ... friendly," Grace said.

"Then you must know Harper," he said as he looked around the room. "You'd think your best friend would come see you in the hospital, not to mention your assistant."

"I thought you fired her," I reminded him.

"Come on, get real. I fire Deidra at least three times a month," he said dismissively. "Where's Harper?"

"He's here," I told him.

Emerson looked around. "Funny, I don't see him."

"I mean he's in the hospital, too. He's in the intensive care unit. Someone tried to poison him," I told him.

"So, they tried to get him too," was all that Emerson would say, which was certainly not what I'd been expecting from him.

"Then you *know* that someone tried to run you into a tree earlier today?" I asked.

"Is that what happened? I didn't know, but I figured I didn't end up here by accident."

"You don't remember what happened at all?" Grace asked him.

He frowned before he spoke. "The truth is that it's all kind of fuzzy. The last thing I remember is Harper asking me to be his best man this morning after we signed some documents for his guy. I thought he was nuts for getting married, but hey, everybody's entitled to their own poison." His frown worsened into an open scowl as he added, "Strike that. I need to come up with a better phrase."

"We heard about the insurance policy," I told him. "What brought that on?"

"I have no idea. Maybe it was mine, maybe it was his," Emerson said. "You'll have to ask Harper or maybe even Nicholas Southerland. He's Harper's guy for insurance."

"So you didn't know about it beforehand?" I asked.

"I don't remember. Part of me doesn't think I knew about it, but I can't really be sure right this second." He looked around the room again. "I still can't believe Deidra's not here."

"She was, but she got thrown out of the hospital," Grace told him.

He looked at us both oddly, and then he asked, "Is that true?"

"We saw it happen," I admitted.

"Why?"

"Jenny Wilkerson came here with some flowers and said she wanted to see you," Grace answered with a broad smile.

"And Deidra had a problem with that," I finished.

He shook his head in disgust. "I told Jenny it was over last night. Why was she even here?"

"She seemed to think you two were still an item," I supplied.

"After what her husband said to me? No thank you. Vance told me that if I ever got within a hundred yards of his wife again, he'd kill me. I didn't even risk breaking up with Jenny in person; I gave her a call and ended things over the phone."

"How did she take the news?" I asked him.

"Well, she didn't try to send me flowers, if that's what you're asking," he said. "I don't get it."

"She's in denial," I said. "Do you think she was mad enough to run you off the road today?"

"Oh, yeah, she or that crazy husband of hers. I'm still having a hard time believing that's what happened."

"It is, at least according to the police," I said. "There was an eyewitness who saw the whole thing, but they couldn't identify the vehicle that hit you or anyone in it either."

"Man, I've got to start using a little better judgment when I look for female companionship," Emerson Glade said wryly.

"Maybe you should try someone who's *not* married next time," Grace suggested.

"Hey, to each his own." After a moment, he said, "I really need to see Deidra."

"Why, are you going to ask her out?" I asked him.

"What? No! That's *never* going to happen. She's like my kid sister. I told her that last night after she heard me dumping Jenny. She tried to put the moves on me; can you believe that? Claimed that we belonged together. I told her she'd lost her mind, and she stormed out like she was on fire."

"You're one of a kind, aren't you?" I asked him, my voice dripping with sarcasm.

"I do my best," he said a bit smugly. This guy clearly didn't get it.

"Now we know why two people might want to see you die in a car wreck. Care to explain why Thomas Roberts might want you dead?" I asked.

"That's none of your business," he answered curtly. "Is there a nurse around here or something? I'm thirsty."

"I'll go get you one," Grace said as she glanced at me.

Once she was out of the room, I said, "Emerson, we know all about Thomas Roberts believing you and Harper cheated him out of a million dollars."

He got agitated about that, and his monitor started to intensify a bit. "None of that is true!"

"Then set the record straight," I prompted him.

"First of all, it was more like eight hundred grand, nine tops, and second of all, he sold that land to us *way* below market value. Nobody twisted his arm." He paused a moment and then added with a slight smile, "Well, not very hard, anyway."

"You should probably be taking this a bit more seriously," I told him. "After all, somebody tried to kill you *and* your partner today."

"The operative word there is 'tried,'" he said. "Give me your phone."

"Why?" I asked without complying. I wasn't in the mood to take orders from this man. I had known him less than ten minutes, but it had taken quite a bit less than that for me to know that I didn't like him. He was what I hated most about some businesspeople: rude, arrogant, entitled, and demanding. I was fairly certain that my mother could buy and sell him ten times over, and yet she never resorted to behavior like he was exhibiting.

"Because I said so," he replied, which was a grade schooler's answer if ever there was one.

I was about to refuse him again when Deidra hurried into the room with Grace close on her heels. "You're awake," she said as she rushed to his bedside.

"With all that racket out in the hallway, how could I be otherwise?" he asked pointedly.

"I'm sorry about that," she said in a softer voice than I'd heard her use since we'd met. "Jenny came by."

"I heard," he said. "Is she coming back?"

"Not anytime soon," Deidra crowed, and I had to wonder what had transpired between them in the hospital parking lot. I'd have to track Toby down and ask him, but in the meantime, I wasn't finished up here yet.

"Good." Emerson then looked at Grace and me and asked, "What are you two still doing here? Gabby's not here, and since that's the only reason I might be willing to see you, there's nothing left to say."

"If you don't talk to us, I'm sure the police will be glad to question you in more formal circumstances," I said. It was a card we rarely played, but a great many times, it yielded results. After all, most people were much more likely to speak with us than someone in uniform.

"Bring them by," he said and then dismissed us both. "In the meantime, I've got business to conduct, so you need to go."

"You heard the man," I said, turning to Grace. "He wants you to leave."

"I meant *both* of you," he insisted.

Oh, well. It had been worth a shot.

"Where to now?" Grace asked me after we were back out in the hallway. "Should we go check on Gabby again while we're here?"

"No. If we do that, we'll have to explain why we aren't out there trying to find her new husband's attempted killer," I said. "I'd like to see if Jenny or her husband, Vance, have alibis for this morning when the car wreck occurred, and then I'd like to track Thomas Roberts down and see where he was."

"Correct me if I'm wrong, but I was under the impression we were trying to find whoever poisoned Harper Wilcox, not hit Emerson Glade," Grace said. "Not that I'm complaining, but it's a fair question, isn't it?"

"It's totally in line," I answered as we made our way out into the parking lot where we'd left my Jeep. "I just have a hunch that whoever tried to get rid of Emerson is the same person who poisoned Harper."

"Honestly, I've only spent ten minutes with the man, and I could totally see myself running him off the road into a tree on general principles alone."

"Again, that's a fair point," I answered as I hesitated at the Jeep without getting in. "Do you think I'm wrong?"

"No, ma'am. I would never say that," Grace replied in a serious tone.

"But you might think it, right?" I asked her.

"I refuse to answer on the grounds that it's possibly true," she answered.

"Tell you what. Let's spend a few hours on this, and if nothing comes of it, we'll focus on Harper Wilcox again. What could it hurt, right?"

"Hey, I learned long ago not to dispute your gut, Suzanne," she said. "This is going to be fun, isn't it?"

"I'm sure Jenny would love nothing more than to see us again so soon," I told her as I looked over and saw a man and woman arguing in one corner of the parking lot away from everyone else. "It looks as though we're in luck. There's Jenny now, and unless I miss my guess, that man she's arguing with is bound to be her husband, Vance."

Chapter 13

"I DON'T CARE *how* your boyfriend is doing," the man said loudly. It wasn't quite a shout, but it was close enough not to matter. "I'm not sitting here all day waiting around for you."

"That's too bad, Vance. If you expect me to be your chauffeur, then you don't really have any choice," Jenny said, matching him toe to toe.

"You volunteered, remember?" her husband asked her.

"I felt sorry for you. Why, I don't know. You should know better than to drive drunk."

"I was set up!" he protested, growing even more agitated than he'd been before. "They set that checkpoint up a block from my pub."

"Why do you even have a pub? Besides, just because you don't have a license doesn't mean you can't drive. You just can't get caught," she snapped.

"I am not losing my driver's license!" he answered, almost to the point of hysteria.

"Calm down," Jenny cautioned him. "Your blood pressure is off the charts as it is."

"That's what comes from being married to you," he answered in a bit of a grumble.

Grace and I were about twenty feet away from the arguing couple, but they still had no idea that we were there. Even at my worst with Max, I'd never gotten that bad, and neither had he.

"Yeah, well, I didn't complain all morning when I drove you all around Hickory to your meetings, did I? You didn't even thank me!"

"Thanks so very much," he said, his voice dripping with sarcasm. "All I did was buy you the Lexus you had to have. I'm really asking too much for you to do me a favor and drive me around, aren't I?"

"I married you, didn't I?" she asked. "How many favors do you expect?"

"I have come to expect your little indiscretions, Jenny. What I don't like is how you're flaunting this one."

"Well, you don't have to worry about him anymore. I dumped him."

That was news to us, especially since Emerson had just told us that he'd been the one to cut her loose. Oh well, if it helped her sleep at night, what did it matter to me?

"Do you expect me to be grateful for that?" he asked her.

"No, I understand that would be asking too much. It looks like I'm going to be hanging around the house after all."

"I wish I could say how happy that prospect made me, but I hate to lie to you," he answered with a wicked little grin.

"Funny, I thought it had become a habit with you, you've done it so much," she answered.

I'd had enough of their bickering and the story of their unhappy lives together. I touched Grace's arm lightly and motioned her away from the scene.

"Don't you want to stay and see how it turns out?" she asked me.

"I *know* how it turns out," I said. "We got all we needed from them."

"They actually alibied each other without us having to even ask," Grace replied. "That was awfully convenient."

"Maybe a little too convenient," I countered as we headed for my Jeep.

"What are you thinking, Suzanne?"

"Grace, is there any chance that they saw us there all along? Is it possible they put on that little show just for us?"

She appeared to think about it for a few seconds before she spoke again after we got in and closed the doors. "I have a hard time believing they could agree on what to have for dinner, let alone how to cover up for two attempted murders."

"Maybe, just maybe, that's what they want us to believe," I replied.

"Suzanne, you're getting paranoid in your old age, aren't you?"

"I don't have to keep reminding you that we're the same age, do I?" I asked her. Before she could answer, I continued. "I don't know what to think, and what's more, how do we check it out? I doubt we can just start calling businesses in Hickory and asking them if they met with Vance Wilkerson today, can we?"

"No, it's not likely. What does he do for a living?"

"He's in construction, isn't he?" I asked. "Didn't Deidra mention something about that earlier?"

"She said he had contacts in the industry," Grace admitted.

"Then I need to call a friend of mine in Hickory in the trades who might know more about it," I said.

"How do you know someone all the way in Hickory?" she asked me as I started going through my cell phone numbers, looking for Carl Spoon's contact information.

"He's a happy customer at my shop, what can I say?" I told her.

"So much so that you have his phone number?" Grace asked.

"I was thinking about getting a bid on some work on the cottage, and I just wanted to use folks I knew personally," I admitted.

"Why wouldn't you use your mother's people?"

"Grace, believe it or not, I have a circle of friends and contacts myself," I told her a bit huffily.

"Hey, take it easy. I was just asking. What project were you considering?"

"A study for Jake," I admitted. "Then I found out how much it was going to cost, so I dropped the idea."

"I understand that," she said.

I called Carl's number and got his voicemail. "Carl, it's Suzanne Hart, your favorite donut lady. At least I hope I am. Listen, call me when you get a chance. I'm checking up on a guy in the trades named Vance Wilkerson, and I need to know if he was in Hickory today. Bye."

"That was a little flirty, wasn't it?" Grace asked me, frowning, as I put my phone away.

"Grace, he's close to seventy years old, not to mention the fact that he's been married to his wife for fifty years. I was just being myself."

"I know that, and you know that, but are you sure *Carl* knows that?" she asked me with one eyebrow arched.

"He knows it. He's even met Jake," I told her.

"Okay then, you should be fine," Grace said as I started driving. "Where are we going?"

"I thought we might go to Union Square and speak with Thomas Roberts," I said.

"How are we going to approach him?" Grace asked. "Can we pretend to be other people?"

"So let me get this straight. You want to be me, and you want me to be you?" I asked her, being purposefully thick about it.

"I was thinking more along the lines of us being with the FBI or even the North Carolina State Contractors Enforcement Agency."

"Is there such an organization?" I asked her.

"I don't know. Wouldn't you think there would have to be?" she replied with a slight grin.

"Let's just go with the truth," I countered.

"The truth? That we're just a couple of nosy broads who want to ask him personal questions and expect him to answer?"

"Well, I would put it a little more delicately than that," I told her, "but that's the gist of it."

"I like my idea better," she said as I drove.

"I'm sure you do, but let's try it my way, shall we?"

"I still think we need a better cover story than we're just curious," Grace replied.

"You've got a point," I conceded. "We'll tell him that Harper and Emerson both expressed concern that what happened to them might be related to the deal they pulled over on him."

Grace smiled. "In other words, we lie. I like it."

"We don't know that Harper doesn't feel that way, and from what Deidra told us, Emerson surely thinks he might be involved," I said, trying to justify myself.

"Hey, I wasn't criticizing you," she said. "I was congratulating you. I'm still not sure why he'd tell us anything though."

"We can say that we are about to share our suspicions with the police, but we wanted to give him a chance to rebut their claims before we did."

"I like it," Grace said. "One thing, though."

"What's that?"

"Doesn't it kind of put targets on our backs?"

I just shrugged. "Sometimes we have to do that. You should know that by now as well as I do."

"Oh, I get it. I just wanted to make sure that you did."

I thought about it for a second before I answered. "I can handle it if you can."

"You know I'm game for just about anything," she replied.

"Just about?" I asked with a smile.

"Okay, I'll take out the condition. If it's good with you, it's good with me."

I had to laugh at that response. "That's a dangerous promise to make, young lady."

"Hey, I love living on the edge," she replied.

When we got to the address for Thomas Roberts's construction company that Grace had pulled up from her phone, I was surprised to see an old truck sitting in one of the parking spaces in front of the office. From the looks of it, it had been in an accident, and recently from what I could see.

Had we found the person who'd tried to kill Emerson Glade and maybe even his business partner, Harper Wilcox, too?

"Does that look like a new dent to you, Grace?" I asked her as I bent down to examine the scored metal section of the passenger-side front fender. Part of the paint off the white truck had been scraped away, and there were streaks of dark-blue paint from the impact of whatever the driver had hit.

She ran a hand over it. "Absolutely. These old dings over here are rusted over, but this one's fresh."

"That's where it would be if you tried to run somebody off the road, right?" I asked.

"I've never had the pleasure, but it would just about have to be, wouldn't it? Let's say you're following someone, and you decide to make your move. You act as though you're going to pass them on the left, but as you do, you suddenly swerve into them, forcing them off the road. This is exactly where you'd have to strike to make that happen."

"Wow, you came up with that pretty quickly," I told her. "Should I be worried about driving in front of you in the future?"

"Not as long as you're nice to me," she said with an evil grin.

I was about to reply when a tall and burly man came shooting out of the office. As he glared at us, I couldn't help noticing the prominent bandage on his forehead that covered a third of it. He must have taken quite a jolt from whatever had caused it. Say hitting another vehicle, perhaps?

"What are you doing near my truck?" he asked as he stomped toward us.

"We couldn't help but notice you were in an accident recently," I said as serenely as I could with this ogre breathing in my face. "It must have just happened today, from the look of it."

"I did it yesterday," he grumbled, "not that it's any business of yours. Who are you two?"

"We're just a pair of concerned citizens," Grace said. "I'm sure for an accident of that size, you must have called the police *and* the insurance company." She turned to me and said, "It's easy enough to find. I'll have my husband, the chief of police, check into it."

"You talking about the chief here?"

"No, in April Springs," she said serenely. "If my husband can't help us, I'm sure hers would be more than happy to."

"Who's your husband, the mayor or something?" he asked derisively.

"No, he recently left the North Carolina state police as their lead special investigator," I told him. "He's got lots of contacts everywhere."

"Why should you two care, anyway?"

"We happen to know the man you hit," I told him. "Does Emerson Glade ring any bells?"

"That's a lie," he said, sputtering and turning a deep maroon. "I never did any such thing."

"That's not the way it looks to us," I told him. "Listen, we'd be happy to drop it if you'll just tell us what really happened."

"I hit a car on a construction site yesterday. You happy?" he asked begrudgingly. "Not that it's any of your business."

Grace nodded. "I was sure it was something simple."

He looked as though he was happy at the thought of getting rid of us when I added, "We'll just confirm that there was a police report issued and an insurance claim made, and we'll go back and tell them that you didn't do anything." I didn't go into detail about who "they" might be. I'd found over the years that it was better to leave that open ended. Let the bad guy's imagination supply the details. Plus, it didn't commit me to any particular lie.

"We didn't report it. Okay?" he snapped.

"Why on earth wouldn't whoever you hit do that? Unless he didn't know you were the one who struck him."

"He knew all right. He was sitting in the car. Gave me a nasty knot on my forehead when my head hit the steering wheel," Roberts complained as he gingerly touched the bandage on his head. "I gave him some cash to make him forget all about it, and he was happy enough to do it. I can't afford my premium being jacked up any more than it already is. That Southerland guy is as big a crook as his pals Glade and Wilcox are. I never should have given him my business."

"So, you admit that you harbor ill feelings toward Emerson and Harper?" I asked him sweetly. Sometimes it really did pay to kill a suspect with kindness. I was just hoping that this was one of those times.

"Just because I think they're both crooks doesn't mean I'd try to run one down."

"Then you've heard about what happened to Emerson?" I asked him.

"Word gets around," was all that he was willing to admit.

"And Harper?" Grace asked.

"What's wrong with Wilcox?" he countered, and for some reason, I believed that he hadn't heard about what had happened.

"Somebody tried to kill him with poison today," I said.

Roberts just shook his head. "That's a woman's weapon," he snapped. "I'd never do that."

"Unlike a vehicle. That's a lot more manly way to try to kill someone, isn't it?"

"I didn't do either of those things!" he snarled. "Now get off my property before I throw you off. Both of you!"

"Take a step back," Grace said as she reached a hand in her purse. She said it with such calm assurance and firmness that it caught him off guard. The blustering man did as he was told, and he took a few steps back toward the front door of his office.

"You both need to go," he repeated, though this time, his gaze never left Grace's hand, which was still buried in her handbag.

"We're leaving, but that doesn't mean we won't be back," I said. I was probably pushing it, but I found that I rarely got anywhere without being a little more assertive than I was in my regular life.

"Suit yourself, but I won't be this polite next time," he replied before going back inside.

As the door closed, Grace said, "Neither will we."

The door slammed behind him, and I turned to Grace. "Tell me you're not armed."

"Whatever gave you that idea?" she asked as she pulled out a roll of wintergreen Lifesavers and her pepper spray she never left home without.

"You took a real chance implying that you had a gun on you," I told her, though I couldn't hide the hint of admiration I had in my voice.

"It worked this time, so it's all good."

"The key phrase in that sentence is 'this time,'" I told her as I pulled my cell phone out of my jeans pocket and took a few photos of the damaged fender, paint streaks included, and his license plate too, so we'd have some proof in case he decided to get it fixed.

"Now who's the one who's taking chances?" Grace said as she kept looking nervously toward the door. "Suzanne, let's get out of here. I have a bad feeling about that man."

"I'm getting that about most of the men we've been dealing with today," I told her, but I did what she suggested and headed back to the Jeep.

I pulled out and headed down the road. When we got about twenty feet away, I could swear I heard a gunshot behind us!

"Are you okay, Grace?" I screamed out as I took the corner on the next street practically on two wheels.

"Was that really a gunshot?" she asked me as she tried to look back to where we'd just been.

"It sure sounded like one to me," I admitted. "I suppose it could have just been a car backfiring, but for some reason, I don't believe it."

"On second thought, maybe it *was* a bit reckless making him think that I was armed," Grace replied, her voice quivering a bit as she said it.

"We need to watch our backs from here on out," I told her as I headed toward our next destination.

She took note as I skipped the turnoff to April Springs and looked at me as though I'd just lost my mind. "Are you going *back* there, Suzanne?" she asked incredulously.

"No, but we're not finished with Union Square just yet. We still need to speak with Nicholas Southerland."

Chapter 14

"MAYBE WE SHOULD TALK to him tomorrow?" Grace asked me.

I glanced over at her and saw that she was still visibly nervous. Getting shot at, if that was what had really happened, would do that.

"We can't be positive that Roberts shot at us," I told her.

"No, but it doesn't hurt us one bit to act as though that was what happened."

"Would you like me to drive you back to April Springs?" I asked her as I pulled into a laundromat parking lot.

"That depends. Are you coming back here without me?"

"I'm going to follow this last lead," I admitted.

"Then I'm going with you."

"I hate to be stubborn," I said as I pulled out, "but time is a factor here."

"I'll be okay, Suzanne. I just needed a minute."

I glanced over at her again, and she did seem as though she'd calmed down some. "It's not always cupcakes and daisies investigating these things, is it?"

"I'd go so far as to say it's never that," she answered, "but it still beats someone getting away with attempted murder. Twice."

"I agree," I said. "What was that address again?"

She checked her phone and then directed me to Southerland's business.

I was relieved to see two cars parked out front when we got there, but I hoped he wasn't with a client and that the other car belonged to his secretary.

We were in luck.

That was how we found things when we walked in.

But that was about all of the luck we had.

"I'm sorry, but I'm not going to discuss my clients' arrangements with you," Nicholas Southerland told us once we were shown into his office. The short, thin, balding man had been all sunshine and smiles when he'd thought we were looking for personal policies for ourselves, but once we asked the first question, a wall had gone up across his face.

"Aren't you the least bit concerned that two men you wrote life insurance policies for over the past two days are *both* in the hospital?" I asked him.

"That's pure coincidence," he said.

"Is the home office going to see it that way too, I wonder?" Grace asked him.

I think he flinched a bit, but I couldn't be sure. There was no way I'd ever get into a poker game with this man.

"Or are the policies not in effect yet?"

"As of midnight yesterday and nine a.m. today, respectively, they were active," he admitted, "but that's all you're getting from me without written permission from my clients, and from what I understand, neither of them is capable of doing that at the moment."

"I bet we could get something from Emerson," Grace said. "He's awake, by the way."

"We could, but actually, we don't need him." I turned to Southerland. "Do you have a fax machine?"

"Of course."

I pulled out my cell phone and said, "I'm calling Gabby. She is going to have one major fit when I tell her that she's going to have to fax permission to Mr. Southerland here to get him to answer any of our questions, but that's on him." I then turned to the insurance man and said, "I wouldn't want to be in your shoes in about ninety seconds."

He absolutely flinched that time, but who could blame him? I'd been on the receiving end of more than one of Gabby's tantrums, and it wasn't a pleasant experience, to say the least.

"If you can get her verbal consent on the telephone, that should suffice," he answered as I said hello and put the call on speaker.

"Gabby, it's Suzanne. How's Harper?"

"No change," she said tersely. "Are you two making any progress?"

"We're trying, but we're getting stonewalled by some of the folks involved."

"Give me names and numbers, and I'll take care of them," she said angrily. Clearly, my friend needed some way to vent her frustration, and I had just given her the perfect excuse to lose her cool.

"Ms. Williams, it's Nicholas Southerland here," the agent said.

"It's Mrs. *Wilcox*," Gabby insisted. "I don't know how long I'm going to be able to call myself that, but while my husband is still drawing breath, that's my name. Are you giving my representatives difficulties, Nicky? Do you really want to jeopardize all of the business you do with my husband and his partner by aggravating me?"

"Of course not," he spoke up quickly. "I just needed to be sure that I could discuss confidential matters with your, ah, associates."

"Well, you can, so go ahead," she snapped. "Suzanne, I've got to go. That nice young nurse is motioning over to me."

"Keep me posted," I said, but it was just to dead air. I wondered if she was about to get some good news or some bad, but either way, there was nothing I could do for her at the moment from so far away.

"There. Are you satisfied?" I asked him after I put my phone away.

"To a degree," he admitted. "I'm afraid I can't discuss Mr. Glade's situation or any and all arrangements that might or might not have been made with Mr. Wilcox despite Mrs. Wilcox's assurance that it was acceptable."

Grace turned to me and asked, "Did he go to law school, do you think? He sure sounds like a lawyer to me."

I decided to ignore her jab at the man, though she had a point. It was obvious that Nicholas Southerland was a man used to covering his own rear end. "Tell us about the policy between Gabby and Harper," I told him.

"It's a standard life insurance policy, reciprocal, paying out one million dollars upon the death of one of the signatories."

"And you told us earlier that it was already in effect. Isn't there some kind of waiting period for a policy of that size to take effect?" I asked him.

"Ordinarily, yes, but we've done a great deal of business with Mr. Wilcox and his associates over the years, and my superiors approved the institution of the policy immediately, at Mr. Wilcox's request—insistence, actually."

"He was eager to get the paperwork signed?" I asked pointedly.

"Most assuredly," he replied.

"Does that go for the policy with Emerson as well?" I asked.

"As I said before, I won't discuss that with you."

"Fine," I said. "Why the rush though? Do you have any idea?"

"It's not my job to understand the motives of my clients," he said primly, and then he added, "Though I've seen in the past that when people undergo major lifestyle changes, they tend to focus on making these sorts of arrangements. It was clear to me from our prior conversation that Mr. Wilcox wanted to ensure that his wife and business partner would both be taken care of if something happened to him."

"Why would he think that something was about to happen to him?" Grace asked intently.

"I couldn't say," Southerland replied.

"Can't or won't?" Grace pushed.

He merely shrugged in response, and I had a hunch he was already regretting what little he'd told us.

I was about to ask him a follow-up on Harper's state of mind when the secretary popped her head in. "I'm sorry to interrupt you, Mr. Southerland, but Mr. Washington is here for his appointment, and he's threatening to leave if you won't see him right now."

Nicholas Southerland stood and walked to the door. "I'm afraid that's all of the time I've got for you ladies. Have a good day."

It was an obvious brush-off, and I could see Grace's spine stiffen in rebuttal, but I touched her arm lightly and shook my head. "Thank you for your time, Mr. Southerland."

"Always happy to help a client or their *representatives*," he said, putting a sarcastic spin on the last word.

Once we were back outside and sitting in the Jeep, Grace said, "We could have gotten more out of him if we'd kept pushing."

"He regretted telling us what he did," I told her. "Besides, we got plenty."

"You think?" she asked.

"I do. Why would Harper be worried about what would happen to Gabby or Emerson all of a sudden?"

"You heard the man. He was getting married, and he felt as though it was time to reassess how well the people in his life would be protected if something happened to him."

"That's the thing though," I said as I pulled out of the parking lot and headed back toward April Springs.

"What are you thinking, Suzanne?" she asked me.

"I'm just wondering if this poisoning was the *first* attempt on Harper Wilcox's life. If something happened earlier, he might have just been trying to make sure that Gabby and Emerson were both left in good shape, at least financially, if whoever was trying to kill him actually succeeded."

"We need to talk to Gabby," I said as I started the drive back. We'd actually have to pass through town before we made it to the hospital, since it was on the way to Maple Hollow and we were just leaving Union Square. When we got into town, we'd be on Viewmont Avenue, which dead-ended into Springs Drive, which became the road to the hospital. "Do you mind delaying getting home a bit?"

"No. Stephen's going to be digging into this case, and besides, we aren't exactly on cordial terms at the moment. Then again, it's not a night when we're supposed to see each other anyway, so I'm going to catch up on paperwork tonight."

I knew better than to say anything.

But I did it anyway.

"Grace, he has a right to have ambition," I told him. "So what if he wants to be a state cop?"

"That's not all of it," Grace told me. "Are you sure you want to talk about this?"

"What else do we have to discuss, besides two attempted murders, I mean?" I asked.

"Do you want to know why I hold your husband partially to blame?"

Things got quiet as I thought over my answer. After a full minute, I said, "Go ahead. Shoot."

"That's a bad choice of words, Suzanne, given what just happened to us."

"I mean you can say anything you want to me," I responded.

"The thing is, Stephen wants to be like Jake when he grows up," she told me.

"He's already grown up," I countered.

"You know what I mean. Your husband has made his life as a state police special investigator so glamorous that Stephen wants to do it, too. Isn't there *anything* you can do?"

"I suppose I could ask Jake to tell him the reality of just how dangerous the job really is," I offered. "After all, he retired at a fairly early age, which is not that uncommon in that job. The stress and the state of constant danger are killers, so if the bad guys don't get you, your own body attacks you with a heart attack or something equally bad."

"He knows all of that," Grace said with a sigh.

"How about this?" I asked her. "Jake has some friends still on the job. Maybe if Stephen heard from some of them, he might realize what he's trying to get into."

"It might be worth a shot. Just have him find people who are burned out though. I have an even better idea," she said suddenly. "You mentioned that other people have retired early. Let Stephen talk to *them* about the stresses and strains."

"I don't know. It might work," I offered.

"Let's face it. It probably won't, but at least I'll know that I've done everything in my power to talk him out of taking on a more dangerous job than the one he's got right now. I'm just getting used to being married. I don't want to have to get used to being a widow."

"I understand completely," I told her.

"Good. That's settled then."

"Does that mean that then you'll forgive Jake, no matter what happens?" I asked her. Honestly, it was too much of a strain for me to have my best friend and my husband at odds, and I didn't like it.

"Provisionally," she said, and then she smiled slightly. "Oh, fine. He's off the hook, and so are you. Stephen is going to be Stephen, but I do want you to ask Jake to give it one more try."

"Consider it done," I told her. "Now, how are we going to approach Gabby once we get to the hospital?"

"You're asking *me*? You're her best friend, not me," Grace said, a bit appalled by me even asking her for advice.

"I guess I was just looking for an easy answer," I admitted.

"The only advice I can give you is to ask her point-blank. That's the best way *anyone* can deal with Gabby Williams."

"Gabby Wilcox," I corrected her automatically. It would take some getting used to calling her by her new name, but if she was going to do it, then so could I.

"Call her by whatever name you'd like, just as long as I don't have to be the one asking her if somebody's been trying to kill her new husband."

"Fair enough," I said.

We were still ten minutes from getting to April Springs when my phone rang. I handed it to Grace. "Put it on speaker."

Once she did and I saw who it was, I said, "Hey, Carl. Thanks for calling me back."

"Suzanne, you should know that my wife heard that message," Carl said, his voice a bit grim.

"Was she upset that I was calling you?" I asked, wondering if there was a chance in the world that Grace was right, that I'd been flirting with Carl Spooner without even realizing that I was doing it.

"She was," he said.

"I am so sorry. I didn't mean to cause trouble between you," I confessed.

"Well, she said the next time you want to speak with me, you do it in person. She also mentioned that it wouldn't hurt if you brought a dozen donuts with you, too. I was just pulling your leg, Suzanne. What's got you so paranoid?"

It was a relief to hear that he'd just been teasing. "I was worried I was making things bad for you at home."

"Please, my wife knows I love her more than the very breath I take," he said.

"My, that's awfully poetic for a builder," I told him. "You're a real romantic, aren't you?"

"You know what I always say. It takes a real stud to build a house. Now, about that question you asked me in your message."

"I know it's a long shot, but I had to ask," I said. "If you don't know him, or you didn't see him this morning, it's fine."

"Suzanne, will you let me answer? The truth of the matter is that I happened to be meeting with Vance at noon today."

"Are you sure about the time?" I asked him. If Vance and his wife were in Hickory at noon, there was no way he could have run Emerson Glade off the road earlier, let alone try to poison Harper Wilcox a little later.

"Dead certain. I walked him out so I could have lunch with my wife. I never miss it if it's humanly possible."

"Did you happen to see if Vance was alone?" Grace asked him.

"Who might that be asking questions now?"

"Sorry, it's Grace Gauge. Actually, I'm Grace Grant, one of Suzanne's friends."

Grace never identified herself as Stephen's wife, and I had to wonder if Gabby's new moniker had given her pause to reconsider her earlier choice. I was Suzanne Hart at the donut shop, and the bank for that matter, but there were times I was happy to be Suzanne Bishop.

"The chief's wife?" he asked.

"The very same," she admitted.

"He's a good man, or so I hear," he said. "Now, getting back to your question, as a matter of fact, Vance's wife was with him. She was driving him around like some kind of taxi driver, and from the expression on her face, she was none too happy about it."

That alibied Vance and his wife, Jenny. We had to mark them off our list as suspects in both cases we were investigating.

"Thanks, Carl. You've been a real peach," I told him.

"Enough to get a free donut the next time I come to town?" he asked with a laugh.

"Tell you what. I'll give you one and one to take home to your wife."

"I'll see you tomorrow then," he answered.

"You don't have to make a special trip. Those donuts will be waiting for you whenever you want to claim them," I told him with a grin.

"Then maybe the day after," he said, and then, without another word, he hung up.

"I wonder what his business was with Vance Wilkerson?" Grace asked.

"I don't know. Is it relevant?"

"Suzanne, you know as well as I do that we don't know what's relevant until we figure it all out," she answered.

Without a word, I reached over and dialed Carl's number again.

"Listen, if you keep calling me, my wife might get jealous after all," he answered. I could hear the grin in his voice, but I still didn't want to make a habit of it.

"What did Vance want with you, or is that some kind of privileged information?" I asked him.

"It might be to him, but it's not to me," he answered. "He was looking for work, truth be told."

"I thought he was some kind of big-time wheeler-dealer," I said.

"He likes to think so, but I have a hunch he's scraping by, just like most of us. You wouldn't believe some of the whispers I hear about contractors living on the edge of bankruptcy around these parts."

"You're not in danger of going under, are you?" I asked him, legitimately concerned for my friend.

"No, ma'am. Not me. I buy old trucks and equipment and fix them up. Some guys buy new everything, spend money like it's going out of style, and then act surprised when the piper has to be paid. Listen, I'd love to chat, but my wife is waiting for me, and that is one woman I don't want to disappoint. See you around."

"So that doesn't help after all," Grace said after the call was over.

"Like you said, we don't know what matters until we have the answer. In the meantime, I need to prepare myself to speak with Gabby about one of the most uncomfortable subjects I've ever had to discuss with her."

"Yeah, good luck with that," Grace answered. "If you don't mind, I might just wait for you in the Jeep."

"You could at least come in," I told her.

"Okay, but I'm not taking a step past the lobby. Take it or leave it."

"I'll take it," I said.

"Stephen, what are you doing here?" Grace asked her husband when we walked into the hospital lobby.

"I was checking on the two patients," he said, "but since you're here, we really need to discuss this, and I won't take no for an answer this time."

"Fine. You want to talk? Then by all means, let's talk," Grace said, the determination plastered across her face.

Stephen definitely had the expression of being careful what he wished for, but he led her over to one of the benches in the atrium while I went off in search of Gabby.

Everything considered, I was suddenly happy about the task I had ahead of me and not Grace's. Gabby was definitely the lesser of two evils at that moment.

Chapter 15

"HE'S IMPROVING!" GABBY said excitedly as I walked into the ICU waiting room. "Isn't that amazing?"

"That's excellent news. May I speak with him?" I asked her.

"I said he was getting better, not that he was fully recovered," she corrected me. "He's not even out of the woods yet, but they just told me that they are hopeful that he's responding to the treatment." She hugged me, something that was definitely uncharacteristic for her, and added, "Thank you so much, Suzanne."

"I'm always here for you, Gabby," I told her.

"That's not what I'm talking about, and you know it. Scuttlebutt around the hospital is that you found the poison that was used on Harper, and that Dr. Liar didn't have a clue, even though he's taking all of the official credit. I know the truth though, and so do a lot of other people."

"Grace was with me, too," I told her, trying to get some of the love sent her way.

"She might have been with you, but *you* were the one who found it," Gabby answered.

So much for that attempt.

"Gabby, if I can't speak with him, may I speak with you about something? I need to warn you that it's a bit sensitive."

"Suzanne, right now, you've got a free pass. Ask me anything you'd like to know, and if I can, I'll answer you as honestly as possible."

Wow, that was some kind of blank check, and I wondered if maybe I should use it for something a bit more personal, but I couldn't bring myself to do it. I was still trying to find out who had poisoned her new husband and possibly run his business partner off the road as well. "Has anything unusual happened to Harper in the last few weeks?"

She looked at me oddly. "What kind of question is that? How could I possibly know?"

I pushed harder, and I realized that I was going to have to be a bit more specific if I expected to get an answer. "I'm wondering if there have been any other attempts on his life lately."

Gabby looked instantly troubled, and I wondered if I was about to get a lecture, but instead, she looked at me carefully and asked, "How did you know?"

"I didn't," I admitted. "I was guessing, but it seems as though I was right. What happened?"

"He nearly died last week when the exhaust fumes from the portable heater in his construction trailer malfunctioned. If one of his crew hadn't wondered where he was and checked on him, he could have died. It just seemed like an accident at the time. The exhaust hose got pinched accidentally."

"Or accidentally on purpose," I said. "Gabby, I think somebody might be trying to get rid of Harper and Emerson."

"That was an accident this morning," she said, and then she bit her lower lip and frowned. "Or was it?"

"That's what Grace and I were wondering. We spoke with Deidra, on your recommendation."

Gabby seemed to shiver a bit at the mention of the woman's name. "What did you think of her?"

"She's chilling, but we met someone who clearly scared her," I told her.

"I'm not even sure I want to know who could do that," Gabby answered. "You know what? If it's tied into what happened, I want to know."

"Jenny Wilkerson," I said.

"Emerson's mistress," Gabby said.

"Evidently his *former* mistress," I corrected her.

"He actually ended it with her?" she asked me, clearly surprised by the admission.

"Last night," I said.

"Then she must have done it," Gabby replied as she started for the door.

"Where are you going?" I asked.

"To find Jenny," she answered angrily.

"There's no need. We know for a fact that she didn't do it, and neither did her husband."

Gabby frowned at me. "How could you possibly know that?"

"Jenny and Vance were in Hickory all morning in meetings, so they couldn't have run Emerson off the road or poisoned that drink, either," I told her.

"And you have irrefutable proof of that?"

"I have it from a source that I trust as much as I do you," I told her.

"Okay, that's good enough for me then. Who else could it have been?"

"We're looking hard at Thomas Roberts right now."

"Thomas? I knew there was some bad blood about a deal that went south for him, but I don't know if he'd kill Harper and Emerson because of it."

"We went to see him in Union Square," I told her. "He had a dented front right fender on his work truck. The paint was scraped right off of it, and there were some streaks from the car he hit. Added to that, the man was sporting a pretty substantial bandage on his forehead. It was pretty clear it happened during the accident."

"Did you ask him about it?" Gabby asked.

"He claims he hit a car on a construction site where he was working, but he wouldn't give us the owner's name. He didn't file a report with the police or his insurance company, so there's no way to know if what he told us is true or not. Roberts claims he paid the man off in cash because he couldn't afford another claim on his insurance or another ticket from the police, but it all sounded suspicious to us, so we're going to dig in a little more. I took some photos of his fender if you'd like to see them."

"Of course I would," she said, so I pulled out my phone and brought up the pictures in question. She studied the first one then flipped to the next, a much closer shot. "Can you blow that up any?"

I actually knew how to do that, so I tapped the picture and then used my thumb and index finger to expand the image.

"Suzanne, that paint is blue."

"I know," I said. "So what?"

"The truck Emerson was driving was red. Thomas Roberts couldn't have been driving the truck that ran Emerson off the road this morning."

"Really? How can you be so sure?" I asked, feeling let down that one of our hottest leads might not be a lead at all.

"Emerson Glade drives red trucks and *only* red trucks. The first truck he bought as a teenager was red, and he won't buy another one that's not. He considers it some kind of superstitious good luck charm."

"That's too bad," I said, knowing that our one lead was now gone. "I suppose we'll have to mark Roberts's name off our list too."

"Sorry. I didn't mean to cause you any trouble," Gabby said softly.

"Hey, the more folks we can eliminate, the better," I said, trying not to show how much I had been counting on nailing Thomas Roberts as the attempted murderer.

"How about Deidra?" Gabby asked me.

"What about her?" I countered.

"Could she have done it? No, forget that. She's so in love with her boss she'd never harm a hair on his head."

"Ordinarily maybe not, but last night, after he dumped Jenny, Deidra declared her love for him," I told her.

"How did he react to that?"

"He told us that he set her straight, that there could never be anything between them, that she was more like a sister to him."

Gabby's face whitened a bit. "How did she take that news?"

"I don't know, but this afternoon, you'd never know she was upset with him at all. She's protecting him in his room and running errands for him as though nothing happened between them," I said.

"Then she's in denial," Gabby answered.

"Big time. She might have wanted to hurt Emerson last night, but I'm not sure if sleeping on it didn't calm her down a bit. Besides, that doesn't explain why she'd go after Harper, too."

"I'm curious about something, Suzanne," Gabby asked me as she settled back onto the chair that had become her base in the ICU waiting room.

"What's that?"

"I asked you to look into what happened to my husband, not his business partner," she said, clearly straining to keep her tone civil. "Why are you looking into what happened to his partner?"

"I believe that whoever ran Emerson Glade off the road is also the same person who poisoned your husband," I told her. "Find one attempted murderer and find them both."

"I suppose that makes sense," she said, clearly still a bit troubled by it though. "Are you going to focus on Harper now that all of the leads on suspects for Emerson have dried up?"

"We'll dig into Deidra a bit more, but yes, we'll absolutely shift more of our focus to Harper. I don't suppose he's got a secretary who is in love with him too, does he?"

"Vicki Peterson is devoted to her husband, who used to play for the Carolina Panthers. He's a monster of a man, though he's as sweet as could be, but there is not a man alive willing to face his wrath by daring to fool around with his wife, and what's more, everybody knows it. They are well and truly in love, and everybody who knows them is envious of them because of it."

"How does she feel about Emerson?" I asked.

"She seems fine with him, but he's very careful to be proper around her, which she seems to find amusing," Gabby said. "Who else is on your list?"

"How much do you know about Nicholas Southerland?" I asked her.

"*He's* a suspect?" Gabby asked me incredulously.

"Gabby, *everybody's* a suspect until we've eliminated them," I told her.

"Even *me*?"

"*Everybody*," I repeated. I wasn't sure how she would take it, but after a second, she nodded.

"Good. Don't leave any rock unturned," she said.

"Tell me what you know about Nicholas Southerland," I told her.

"Let's see. He and Harper have been doing business for years, so when my husband says, 'Jump,' he asks, 'How high?' Why do you ask?"

"I don't know. He didn't seem all that upset that two men he wrote hefty insurance policies on were both attacked today. That felt a bit odd to me if you want to know the truth."

"Yes, that's not normal behavior," she said.

"Gabby, did Harper say anything about the policies he and Emerson took out on each other yesterday when you got your new policy?"

Gabby considered the question, and then she answered, "My husband told me they were the same policy, that only the names were changed."

"Is there any way I could see a copy of yours?"

Gabby shook her head. "Sorry. They weren't ready yet. We'll have them sometime in the middle of next week."

"I'm surprised you didn't get a copy as soon as you signed it," I pointed out. "Didn't you find that unusual?"

"The entire idea seemed to come to Harper on the spur of the moment," she admitted.

"Really? How odd."

"You keep saying that, Suzanne," Gabby scolded me.

"Well, in cases like these, whenever something seems amiss or out of the ordinary, that's generally a good place to start digging."

"What possible motive would Nicholas Southerland have to kill two men he had just insured for a million dollars each?" Gabby asked me, clearly confused by the prospect.

"I don't know; that's why I want to see the policy."

"I still don't understand."

"Gabby, what if *both* men had died, as was clearly someone's plan? Could there be a clause in those policies that names a third party as the heir if that happened? And could that third party be a confederate the insurance man used? Then again, what if Southerland took both men's signatures and created new policies, outright naming *himself* as the sole beneficiary? There could be a handful of reasons he might not be that upset if those policies were cashed in, especially if there was something in it for him." I was about to follow up as a nurse from the ICU came into the waiting area. She was a different one but not new to me.

"You can see him now, Mrs. Wilcox. He's doing so much better it's amazing," she told Gabby. "Hey, Suzanne."

"Hey, Becka," I said, returning her greeting.

"I've got to go," Gabby said as she stood. "If there's anything else you need, you know where to find me. Don't hesitate to ask, no matter how troubling the question might be."

"I can do that," I said.

I wanted to ask Becka more about Harper's condition, but she didn't linger. It was just as well. Chances are she wouldn't have been able to tell me. The rules and regulations around patients had gotten much stricter over the years, which was fine by me. I didn't want the world to know if there was anything wrong with me, so I tried to respect other people's privacy when I could.

Unless I was investigating a murder or even an attempted one.

Then all bets were off.

Grace was waiting for me when I came into the lobby.

"I was about to come and get you," she said as I joined her.

"You could have, you know."

"And face Gabby? I don't think so," she replied.

"How did it go with you?" I asked hesitantly.

"You first," she insisted.

"Okay. I asked Gabby if anything odd had happened to Harper lately, and she told me that last week, he almost died from carbon monoxide poisoning in his construction trailer. Evidently, the vent hose got accidentally pinched, though it's hard to prove that it wasn't done on purpose."

"That's interesting," she said. "Anything else happen to him?"

"Not that Gabby knew about, but we won't know for sure until we can interview Harper."

"If we ever get to," Grace answered. "How is he? Has there been any change?"

"He's actually taking a turn for the better," I replied, happy to share some good news for a change of pace. "Gabby appreciates what we did, finding that poison in time. It appears that everybody knows we found it and not Dr. Jacobs, so we're getting all of the credit."

"You mean *you* are," Grace corrected me.

"What makes you say that?"

"I know Gabby," she answered with a wry grin. "Anyway, I'm happy he's doing better."

"So am I. I asked if we could speak with him, but she said he's still not in any condition to be interviewed by anyone. I'm guessing that's us and the police, so we'll have to wait and see."

"Then I suppose we'll have to do just that. Where does that leave us?"

"Gabby told me that the only vehicle Emerson will drive has to be red."

"The paint scrapes we saw were blue though," Grace replied.

"Right, so his name has to come off our list, as much as I hate to admit it. At the moment, we're out of active suspects, with the possible exceptions of Nicholas Southerland and Deidra Lang."

"Why would the insurance agent kill them?" she asked me.

"I'll tell you on the drive home," I promised. "In the meantime, what's up with you and Stephen?"

She looked unhappy that I'd brought it up, but I wasn't about to back down.

"It's complicated."

"What part of marriage isn't?" I asked her. "Go on, I'm listening."

Grace shrugged. "I suppose you are right. After all, I don't know what it could hurt to talk about it."

"You never know," I told her. "It might even help."

"Maybe," she said, and then after letting out a sigh, she added, "First of all, you don't have to say anything to Jake. He doesn't have to do anything to dissuade Stephen from joining the state police."

"Does that mean that you already managed it on your own?"

"I wouldn't go that far," she replied. "He's agreed to put his plans on hold for now, but he told me that just because he's delaying the decision doesn't mean that he's given up on the idea. The truth is that he wants more experience before he applies, something Jake has been trying to convince him that he needs all along. You know my husband though. He wants what he wants when he wants it."

I grinned at her. "As opposed to the rest of us, who are all perfectly content with delaying gratification."

"I know, as soon as I said it, I realized how ridiculous it sounded. I told him what I wanted and what I was afraid of, and he listened carefully and took it into account. You know, since he's become our chief of police, he's really matured in ways that sometimes surprise me, even though he is my husband."

"Maybe that should be *especially* because he's your husband," I told her.

"What does that mean?"

"Grace, you set a high bar for yourself, even though you pretend otherwise. Why shouldn't you hold the man you love to the same standards?"

She shrugged. "You never had any trouble meeting them."

"That's because I'm delightful," I told her and smiled broadly.

She laughed at the overexaggeration. "No one could deny that."

"So, how are things between you now? Did talking clear the air any?"

"It did, and I'm glad we spoke, but frankly, I'm tired of thinking about it, let alone talking the subject to death. We've called a one-year moratorium on any major changes in our lives so we can both catch our breath."

"That sounds like a good policy," I agreed, "but it's still something you're probably going to have to deal with somewhere down the road."

"Tell you what, I'll let future Grace take care of that and let her handle the stress and worry," she answered. "Now, can we get back to talking about our case? Or should I say cases?"

"I still believe they're related," I told her, "so let's just call it one case with two different actions."

"We can call it whatever makes you happy," she said. "Let's just see if we can solve it."

"I agree, but I'm not sure what else we can do today. Do you mind if we break our investigation for now and start fresh tomorrow after I close Donut Hearts?"

"Honestly, that sounds great to me," Grace answered. "I've had about enough to deal with today. It will be nice putting it on hold for now."

"Is it going to be awkward at home for you?" I asked her as we headed for the parking lot.

"Not at all," Grace replied. "Remember, I told you that I'll be alone tonight. This is one of the nights we were planning on spending apart anyway. Stephen will be at his place, and I'll be at mine. Is Jake home waiting for you?"

"I hope so," I told her.

"You really do love him, don't you?"

"More than I can say," I admitted. "That doesn't mean that everything's always perfect, though. Marriage takes work."

"I know, right?" she asked. "Why don't they put *that* in the brochure?"

"Afraid no one will do it, probably." I laughed.

"That's fair."

On the drive back to her place, we both carefully avoided referring to the case or the state of her marriage. For most people, skirting the two major topics of the day might be difficult, but Grace and I had such a full history of life experiences with each other, we had no problems filling in the lulls. She was an amazing friend, and I was sorry for the things she was going through, but there was nobody I'd rather have at my side working on this case, and she knew it.

Now if only we could figure out what to do next.

Chapter 16

"IS EVERYTHING OKAY, Suzanne?" Jake asked me after I gave him a hug that was quite a bit longer than normal the second I walked in the door.

"I just needed a little extra tonight," I told him as I finally pulled away.

"It was a tough day, wasn't it?"

"It's hard enough figuring out one case, let alone two," I admitted, "but that wasn't the worst of it. I hated seeing Grace and Stephen at odds, and you and Grace too."

"We're fine," Jake said. "We had a nice little talk after she spoke with Stephen while you were still in with Gabby."

"Funny, she didn't mention that," I told him.

"Hey, we're friends on our own even without you being the string that ties us together," Jake replied as he followed me into the kitchen. "Have you eaten yet?"

"To be honest with you, it completely slipped my mind," I answered. "I can whip something up for us. Give me a minute."

"You don't have to," Jake announced as he moved to the refrigerator.

"Jake, I love you with all of my heart, but I don't think I could take a batch of your chili right now. Is that okay with you?"

"I wasn't going to offer you any," he said, "but it's good to know how you feel about my food." I started to protest when he stopped me with a laugh. "Suzanne, I was just kidding. Anyway, neither one of us has to cook. Your mother made extra meatloaf and all of the fixings, so all we have to do is warm it up and enjoy it."

"I love my mother so much," I replied as Jake brought out the Tupperware containers and we each started fixing our own plates. There was a constant stream of containers, mostly going from Momma's place to ours, but every now and then, I'd cook extra and return the favor. My cooking wasn't up to her level, but it was still pretty good, and I knew that sometimes, she just liked eating a home-cooked meal that she herself didn't have to make.

As we finished warming everything up, Jake said, "Tell me about your day."

If Max had said it when we'd been married, he would have appeared to listen but actually just been preparing what he was going to say next. Jake truly listened, and it was one of the most valuable traits a spouse could have, at least as far as I was concerned.

"Do you want to hear about the cases first or Grace and Stephen?" I asked him.

"Dealer's choice," he answered as he put his plate in the microwave and nuked it on half power. "But remember, Grace and I have already talked about what's going on with them."

"I have a question for you about that," I said as I waited my turn.

"I'll answer it if I can."

"Why would Stephen want to leave a job he's just getting good at to tackle something that might be over his head?"

Jake ran a hand through his hair before he answered. "It's like this. He knows there's a huge world of law enforcement out there that he wants to be a part of. I tried to tell him that the glamour is highly overrated and the danger is more than it's worth, but he wouldn't listen to me."

"Evidently, he listened a little bit," I said. "After all, he's staying on as our chief of police for another year."

"That might not have had much to do with what I had to say," Jake admitted.

"You don't give yourself enough credit," I rebutted.

"So you say, but I had a word with an old friend who shall remain nameless, and I was told in no uncertain terms that was the advice he got from my source with the state police."

"So then he isn't doing this just for Grace?" I asked as we traded our plates in the microwave. "Go on and eat while yours is still hot."

"I can wait," he said. "Don't be so hard on Stephen. He could have applied and might even have gotten in, but he felt as though putting it off a year was better for everyone involved but particularly for his marriage."

"I can live with that," I said as I nodded.

"I'm sure he'll be thrilled that you approve," Jake replied with a slight grin. "Now, tell me about the cases you've been working on."

"You've been helping the police, so I'm sure you know more than I do at this point," I told him.

"Maybe, but I'm not allowed to share what I know with you. Besides, once some of the preliminary work was done, the chief told me that he had it covered and sent me on my way."

"Really?"

"Yes, he said something about needing to get rid of his training wheels, so I decided to give him some space."

"So what did you do with the rest of your day?" I asked.

"I spent some time hanging out with George," Jake admitted.

"What's the mayor up to that he needs a state police special investigator?"

"I was there more as a friend," he said. "I ran into him downtown, and we started talking. The next thing I knew, your mother was calling me with these leftovers ready to be put away, so I hightailed it over there before she could change her mind."

"You've really made a home here, haven't you?" I asked him as I took a bite of Momma's delicious meatloaf.

"I hope so," he answered as he looked around our cottage.

"I mean in April Springs," I told him. "Sometimes it feels as though you've lived here all of your life."

"Really? It doesn't feel that way to me at all," Jake admitted.

I got a bit concerned hearing that. "Aren't you happy here, Jake?"

He leaned over and took my hand in his. After giving it a brief squeeze, he said, "Wherever you are is where I want to be, whether that's the mountains, the beaches, or anyplace in between."

I reached over and kissed him. "For a cop, you say the sweetest things sometimes."

"An ex-cop," he reminded me, as he was wont to do.

"Do you miss it terribly?"

"Sometimes, but then I can always count on you to bring a bit of that world back into my life."

"I don't dig into that much crime, do I?" I asked, knowing full well that the answer was yes.

"I'd say that it's just about the right amount," he replied, and then he took another bite of dinner. "Go on. Talk to me."

Once I brought him up to date on everything Grace and I had done that day related to Harper's poisoning and Emerson's attempted vehicular homicide, he frowned a bit without speaking.

"Did I do something you don't approve of? I know Grace and I don't use accepted police methods in our investigations, but you have to admit that we manage to get results."

"It's not that," he said. "Hang on a second. I need to grab my phone."

"Who are you calling? I'm guessing that you already thanked Momma for the food."

"This is something a bit more important than that," he said.

When he came back with his cell phone, he hit the speaker function, and I was surprised to hear Stephen Grant's voice on the other end.

"I was just about to call you," Stephen said. "I've been talking to Grace about what she and Suzanne did this afternoon."

"Same here. Are you thinking what I'm thinking?" Jake asked him.

"If you're thinking that I need to post guards outside Harper's and Emerson's rooms tonight, then you sure are. There's a problem, though."

"What's that?" Jake asked. "By the way, you're spot on as to why I was calling you."

"My department doesn't have anything left in the budget for overtime," Stephen admitted.

"So that means what exactly?" Jake asked him.

"Which guy do you want to guard tonight, Harper or Emerson?" Stephen asked with a hint of laughter in his voice.

"You pick," Jake replied. "I'll pick you up in a minute, if you've already eaten, that is."

"I had some leftover pizza. A minute will be fine, but you might be better off making it two. I'm at my place, not Grace's," he added.

"Everything good there?" Jake asked tentatively. It was about as much prying into other people's personal lives as he was ever willing to do.

"It's fine," he said. "I'll see you in a few."

"I'll be there."

After he hung up, I asked, "Do you really think that both men are still in danger?"

"They're both alive, aren't they? Whoever tried to kill them could easily try again," Jake answered as he started clearing away his plate and glass.

"You can't just keep watching them forever," I reminded him.

"That's where you and Grace come in. You two figure out who's behind this, and then we won't have to."

"No pressure or anything, right?" I asked him.

Jake paused a moment to kiss me. "I have faith in you, and I know Stephen has faith in Grace."

"Can you still stay up all night?" I asked indelicately.

"Hey, many is the time I pulled an all-night stakeout when I was on the force," he protested.

"That was quite a while ago though," I reminded him.

"I'll be fine," he answered. "Sorry I'm deserting you tonight."

"Don't be," I told him. "After I finish cleaning up, I'm going to bed. This was a big day, and tomorrow morning is going to roll around soon enough. Stay safe."

"You bet," he said.

I walked him to the door, and there was a distinct pep in his step. I knew that Jake truly came alive when he was being productive, so in a way, I was happy that he'd found some purpose again, if only for one night.

"See you tomorrow."

"You can count on it," I told him.

After he was gone, I did as I'd promised him and finished cleaning up the kitchen before changing and going to bed. It wasn't even all that early for me, though I knew that most folks would never try to go to sleep at that hour. Then again, they didn't have my schedule. Jake loved his investigating, and while I had grown to enjoy it myself, what I really loved to do was make donuts, and tomorrow, I got to start the entire process all over again.

Jake wasn't home when I woke up the next morning a little before two thirty, but I hadn't been expecting him, so it was no big deal. In a way, it was good news. If Jake was still at the hospital, then nothing bad had happened to Harper Wilcox. I got ready for my day by getting dressed and grabbing some cereal before I headed out the door for my short commute to Donut Hearts. I'd heard of writers who liked to brag about their ten-step commutes from their bedrooms to their offices, but mine wasn't much worse than that, and I got to make donuts all day.

I loved the drive, as short as it was. Going down the short section between our cottage and Grace's house, then on past a house that had been empty for what felt like forever, and then over the old tracks, and I was at work.

It gave me a real sense of satisfaction as I unlocked the door and let myself in. Locking it behind me, I flipped on the smaller back lights, turned on the coffee urn, and then headed into my domain, the kitchen. After turning on the massive fryer to give it time to warm up, I did a few housekeeping chores with the books, did a quick inventory to check my supplies, and then I was ready to get started on my first batch of the day, the cake donuts we sold alongside our yeast donuts. A lot of small operations the size of Donut Hearts stuck to one kind of donut or the other, but I knew that my customers liked variety, and truth be told, I'd probably get bored making only one kind of donut day in and day out. After mixing the master batch of cake donut batter, I separated enough into each smaller bowl I'd already laid out in order to create the cake donuts for the day. Most of them were old favorites, like sour cream, old-fashioned, blueberry, and chocolate, but I always kept a bowl out for a flavor that I just felt like making that day. Today's special was going to be zesty lemon, one of my personal favorites. Soon enough, pumpkin donuts would be added to the menu as a seasonal item, replacing my capricious choice, so I wanted a lemon donut before it did.

I was just loading up our fairly new dropper when Emma walked in, right on time. As she hung up her jacket and grabbed her apron, she said, "Is it just me, or is it getting chillier out there?"

"It's that time of year," I said as I started dropping rounds of the old-fashioned donuts into the piping-hot oil.

She glanced at the bowls. "Is that lemon?"

"It is," I admitted. "I had an itch for one."

"Ooh, save one for me, too."

I smiled. "You've got it. You'd think we'd get tired of donuts after all this time, wouldn't you?"

"I don't know about you, but if you're ever not sure if I'm really dead, wave one of your donuts under my nose. If I don't bite it right out of your hand, you can close the lid."

"Wow, on that morbid thought, I think I'll get back to work," I said.

"Speaking of morbid thoughts, can you believe someone tried to poison Gabby and her new husband on their wedding day?"

"Did someone try to poison them both?" I asked her absently, keeping my mind on what I was doing. That oil was hot enough to cause a massive burn, and I always treated it with the respect that it deserved.

"Come on, Suzanne, Dad told me that you and Grace and Jake were all working together to solve the case," Emma said. Her father, Ray Blake, was our local newspaperman, owner and publisher of the *April Springs Sentinel*. He often got his facts wrong, as he had yet again.

"Grace and I are helping Gabby get through a tough time," I said.

"But not Jake?" she asked.

"That depends. Is this for publication, or are you just curious?" We had an agreement that kept her father and his news stories out of Donut Hearts, but sometimes, I had to remind Emma about it.

"Strike that question. It's none of my business," she said contritely.

"No worries," I said as I finished one batch and rinsed out the dropper before I started on the sour cream cake donuts. I'd do the chocolate next, then the blueberry, and finally the lemon, being careful to wash the dropper thoroughly between batches. Normally, that was Emma's job, but I wasn't in the mood to ask her to do it. I'd ice the donuts a bit later, though they were cooling even as I worked.

"I'll do that," she said. When I didn't immediately yield, she added, "Please? I said I was sorry."

"Did you? I must not have heard that part," I answered with a wry smile. It was always difficult for me to stay mad at my assistant, mostly because she was so very much more than that to me.

"You're right. I'm sorry. I was wrong," Emma said.

I handed her the dropper and started icing the old-fashioned donuts on the rack. "Why don't we put that on tape so you don't have to say it every time it happens?"

"Then again, let's don't and say we did," she replied, and we both laughed. The tension was broken, and we could get back to our world of donutmaking, one we loved sharing in the early-morning hours when most of the rest of April Springs was sound asleep.

Ten minutes before we were set to open, my cell phone rang. It was Jake.

"Emma, I need to take this. Would you finish stocking the display cases?"

"You betcha, boss," she said.

"Hang on one second," I told him when I answered his call, and then I unlocked the front door and walked out to the table and chairs we kept in front of Donut Hearts for our hearty customers who liked to dine on their treats al fresco. "Okay, I'm back. Sorry about that."

"Did I call at a bad time?" he asked.

"No, I just didn't want Emma listening in," I admitted. "She started asking me questions about what we were up to earlier, and it made me a little gun-shy."

"Suzanne, you of all people know how pushy Ray Blake can be. Don't blame Emma."

"I'm trying not to, but sometimes it's hard. How was your night?"

"Not very eventful, which is about the best thing I can report," he said.

"And Harper? How is he?"

"It's actually pretty amazing. They've got him up and walking the hallways, if you can believe it. You and Grace really did save his life."

"We got lucky," I said, realizing just how close we had come to missing that empty aspirin bottle in the trash behind Donut Hearts. If whoever had done it had buried the bottle a little deeper or a little better, Harper Wilcox probably wouldn't have made it.

"I'm sorry. What you meant to say was that due to your investigative acumen and skills honed sharp after a number of years, you applied your knowledge and ability and saved the day."

I had to laugh at that. "You missed your calling. You should have been a PR flack."

"No thank you," Jake said. "I'd honestly rather face gunfire than do that."

"I agree, but try not to do that either. So, what does Harper have to say about what happened?"

"He claims he has no idea how the poison was administered. He was fine one minute, and the next, he was passing out in front of his new bride."

"Does he have any idea of who might want him dead?" I asked. "Or have you had much of a chance to talk to him?"

"Are you kidding? The nurse made one lap around the floor with him, and then I took over. Harper threw a fit when I told him I was going wherever he went, but he wasn't exactly in any position to protest. There was no way I was going to let him out of my sight, and I told him so."

"He should be thanking you for being there for him instead of being snippy about it," I said a little tersely.

"No, I get it. Some men are like that. They hate the idea of being fussed over. He wouldn't stop whining about seeing Emerson, so I took him by his room. Stephen met us at the door and told us that he was sound asleep, and we couldn't go in. You should have seen the look on Harper's face. He was like a kid who lost his fire truck! Wow, I don't envy Gabby that marriage, I'll tell you that much."

"Don't forget, Gabby can be a bit testy herself at times," I reminded him.

"At times? Did you actually just say that?" Jake asked me, the shock in his voice evident.

"I stand by what I said," I answered. "How is Gabby taking the news?"

"She was asleep through most of it, and boy, was she upset when she found out that no one woke her to tell her that her husband was ambulatory. She's in with him right now. How do you think I was able to sneak away to call you?"

"I'm glad you did," I said when I saw one of my regular customers coming my way. After glancing at my watch, I said, "It's time to open, so I've got to go. Thanks for calling."

"You bet."

"Are you staying there much longer?" I asked him.

"I'm not going anywhere for the moment, so get back on the case and solve it, woman."

"Well, you've certainly given me extra incentive to figure this out," I answered. "I love you."

"I know, but it's still not as much as I love you," he answered.

Chapter 17

"GOOD MORNING, SUZANNE," Don Smart said as I opened the door for him to let him into Donut Hearts.

"You're up early," I told him.

"As a matter of fact, I haven't been to sleep yet."

"I wanted to say again how sorry I was about your mother," I said.

"Thank you." He looked around and smiled. "She really loved this place. The woman led a full and happy life, and there are worse ways of passing than doing it in your sleep at eighty-eight. She went through a rough patch at the end, and the medical bills were shocking, but she led a good life, and in the end, it gave her more comfort than you can imagine."

"That's about all you can ask for," I said, thinking about some of the folks who'd been murdered that I'd investigated in the past. "What kept you up?"

"I'm Momma's executor," he said.

"That makes sense," I told him. "After all, you lived in town, while your older brother moved away a long time ago. How is he taking it all?"

"He's got both hands out, looking for money," Don said, shaking his head. "He didn't have any time for Momma while she was alive, but boy oh boy, does he care now. He thought he should be her executor, being firstborn and all."

"I know a lot of folks around here still believe in the old 'heir and a spare' policy," I said.

"Yeah, but sometimes the baby of the family is the right choice."

It was hard for me to imagine this man, well into his sixties with silver hair and wrinkles, as the baby. "What can I get you?"

"Let's start with your largest cup of coffee and three donuts," he said as he settled onto a seat at the counter. He placed a briefcase on top beside him.

After I got him his coffee, I asked him, "Which flavors would you like?"

"Surprise me," he said with a grin.

I grabbed a lemon cake, a sour cream cake, and a glazed yeast donut, a power combination that couldn't go wrong. "You seem as though you're in a pretty good mood, given what you're dealing with," I told him.

"Oh, yes," Don said, patting the briefcase as though it was a loyal old dog. "I've been doing a detailed spreadsheet and a report of all of Momma's assets and debts. I've got the entire thing down in black and white. My brother's insisted on a very specific account of everything I've spent and all of the assets Momma had. What I've got here will stand up in any court of law in the land."

"Do you think there might be a legal problem?" I asked him.

"Knowing my brother, I'm counting on it," Don said happily.

"You don't seem too concerned about it."

"That's because I'm not. My greedy brother wants ninety percent of everything. He claims it's his birthright, being firstborn and all, but I'm splitting it right down the middle, fifty-fifty."

"Did your mother have many assets?" I asked.

"Why do you think I'm smiling?" he asked as he took a bite of donut, eating half of it with one swallow.

"So you're going to be rich," I said. I knew I figured prominently in my own mother's will, and what her net worth was even her husband didn't know, but I dreaded the day I found out. I would rather have my mother around than all of the gold in the world, and I made sure that she knew it too.

"Not by any stretch of the imagination," he said, grinning.

"I don't get it," I told him, confused by his apparent delight.

"I spent the last twenty years convincing my mother that she deserved to do the things she wanted, that she didn't owe either one of us a dime. I told her that if she stumbled to the pearly gates after spending her last penny on herself, I'd be a happy man. My brother did his best to persuade her to save everything she had. He tried to make it sound as though he was looking out for her best interests, but the fact was he was trying to preserve his inheritance. Thank goodness she listened to me. She traveled far and wide, always her passion, and she got the most joy out of life a body could before she got too sick to travel anymore."

"What did your brother think of that?" I asked, intrigued by his story.

"He never knew! Mike called her on her birthday and at Christmas, but the rest of the year, he didn't have anything to do with her."

"I can't imagine," I said, knowing how close I was to my own mother. I knew everybody's relationship with their parents was unique, but I was glad about how much a part of my life my mother still was. As overprotective as she could be, I was happy she was there.

"So what's Mike going to do when you split up the inheritance? Do you think he'll sue you?"

"He can try, but the estate will be closed. He can't dispute the facts, and no attorney is going to take his case. Mike's too cheap to pay one outright, and there's nothing to split with a contingency arrangement. He thinks she's got over a hundred grand in the bank and a house that's worth twice that. He would be wrong," Don added with a grin.

"Still, there's got to be *something* left," I said, thinking about how hard it would be to burn through that much money, even though I knew that Don's mother had enjoyed traveling a great deal over that last quarter of her life.

"There is, but just barely," he said. "The house has two mortgages on it, and the bank accounts have nearly been drained from the medical bills. All of her possessions are going to Habitat for Humanity, a cause she dearly believed in. After expenses needed to wrap up her estate, which I've kept to the bare bone, there's less than two hundred dollars to split between us, but the experiences and memories my mother had were worth far more than that. Did you know she rented a flat in Paris for a month every year for the past twenty years, not to mention her other travels? She used to walk the streets along the Seine, taking in the sights and sounds of the city. She also spent extensive time in London, Dublin, Madrid, and Rome; you name a European capital, and chances are she knew it. When she'd come back home, she'd have these amazing stories to share, and I hung on every word."

"I had no idea," I said. "She always told me she was off visiting her cousin Ima."

Don laughed broadly. "That was her little joke with the world. It came about from her telling me a long time ago that 'One day, Ima going to Paris.' I used to remind her that Ima wasn't getting any younger, and then all of a sudden, she started traveling just like she'd dreamed about doing her entire life."

"It sounds amazing," I told him.

"To the world, she appeared to be a rich old widow sitting on piles of money, but the truth was, she was stone cold broke at the end but full of joy."

"I can only hope for that result when I go," I said as I topped off his coffee. I grinned at him as I asked, "What are you going to do with your share of the inheritance?"

Don shrugged, and then he looked around the shop. "You know, Momma loved this place," he said.

"I know she did, and I loved having her here."

Don suddenly reached into his wallet and pulled out a crisp new hundred-dollar bill. "Suzanne, after you take out what I owe you, do me a favor and treat the next few people who come in. Tell them it's in memory of Caroline Smart."

"I'll do you one better than that," I said with a smile of my own. "I'll match your donation, and I'll limit it to folks just buying donuts to eat here, so it lasts longer. What do you say? Let's officially make today at Donut Hearts the Memorial World-Traveling Caroline Smart Life Celebration. How does that sound?"

"It sounds like it's good to have you for a friend," Don said with the hint of a tear in his eye. He finished off the last bite of the last donut and stood. "Well, I've got to get back and finish all of this paperwork so I can send it to my brother via certified mail. I'm not going to send him cash, though. I'm going to write on the check that by cashing it, he agrees that the settlement is final and that he'll have no recourse in the courts if he decides to sue."

"Will he cash it? And is that restriction even legal?"

Don just grinned. "Who knows? Who even cares? It'll be fun for me, so I'm going to do it. Have a nice day, Suzanne."

"You too, Don."

"Why are you giving away free donuts?" the mayor asked as he walked in later.

"I'm not," I told him.

George Morris frowned. "That's not what I heard."

"Somebody paid for them," I explained. "Don Smart decided to do something nice in memory of his mother, so he's treating folks to free donuts while the money lasts."

George nodded. "He was a good son to Caroline. No one can dispute that."

"Well, maybe one person would," I said, remembering what Don had told me about his brother.

"Mike? He's not worth the oxygen he breathes," George said. "I heard the good news about Harper."

"Yes, Jake said he's up and moving around. Word travels fast, doesn't it?"

"In April Springs? You bet it does," the mayor said. "Does he have any idea what happened?"

"Jake said it was all a blur, and the doctor told him that Harper may never get that slice of memory back, even if he did see something. It's a mystery, that's for sure."

George leaned forward. "Jake thinks it could happen again, doesn't he?"

"What makes you say that?" I asked him softly.

"Come on, Suzanne. Before I was the mayor, I was a cop. It just makes sense," he explained.

"I'm not sure how long he can keep it up. Evidently, Harper's bristling at being on a short leash already. He's complaining that every time he turns around, Jake is right there."

"I can't say that I blame him for being upset, but Jake's doing the right thing. Are you and Grace making any progress?"

"Not so you could tell," I told him.

The mayor tried to smile reassuringly. "Don't give up. You'll figure it out."

"You might have too much faith in me, Mr. Mayor."

"No, ma'am. I refuse to believe that. I'm sure I've got just the right amount. Now, how much do I owe you for my coffee and donut?"

"It's courtesy of the Memorial World-Traveling Caroline Smart Life Celebration." I just loved saying that.

"Tell you what. Let me pay for my own, or add what I give you to the fund," George said as he slid a twenty across the counter. It wasn't the first donation we'd gotten since Don and I had set up the fund, and knowing the folks in April Springs, I had a feeling it wouldn't be the last one, either.

"Done and done," I told him. "Thanks for stopping by."

"Just making my rounds," George said with a grin.

The rest of my morning was filled with folks buzzing about the wedding and the subsequent poisoning, but nobody seemed to be too concerned about Emerson Glade's accident. Maybe it was because he didn't live in April Springs, or that it hadn't happened in town, or even due to the fact that Harper's wedding and poisoning made too big a splash for anything else to be noticed.

Whatever the reason, I wasn't about to forget about it. I had a hunch that the poisoning and the car wreck were intertwined, and solving one would solve the other.

I just didn't know where to go next.

I had a nagging feeling in the back of my mind that I had everything I required to solve the case, but I just couldn't put my finger on the facts I needed. Was it true or simply wishful thinking on my part? Only time would tell.

After I closed up the shop for the day, Grace and I would start digging again, and I hoped that something would make the ideas floating around in my head jell into a legitimate answer.

It had happened before, and I knew if I didn't push it, it just might happen again.

Chapter 18

"WOW, WAS IT MY IMAGINATION, or was today harder than yesterday, even though we made a double batch of donuts then?"

"It's called getting older," I told Emma with a smile as I finished running the report off our register at the end of our working day.

"Come on, you're not that old," Emma said as she finished sweeping the floor out front.

"I was talking about both of us," I said.

"Oh, right. That's what I meant, too."

"Liar," I said with a smile.

"You know it," she answered. "All the dishes are done and put away, the kitchen is as clean as I'm going to be able to get it, and it looks as though we have things looking good out here, too."

"It sounds to me as though you are ready to go," I told her.

"Would you mind terribly?"

"Not at all. What's up? Do you have a hot date?"

My assistant frowned for a second before answering. "I wouldn't know what one of those was if it walked up and bit my nose."

"Things still tense between you and Barton?" I asked her.

"As a matter of fact, they're getting better. I'm sure our little talk helped."

"*Our* little talk?" I asked her as I tore off the tape and compared it to my total.

"No, the one he and I had," she told me.

We were spot-on with where we should be, something that always gave me a bit of satisfaction, especially since I'd been running two totals: the one for Donut Hearts and the one for the Memorial World-Traveling Caroline Smart Life Celebration. "I feel a bit bad profiting from Don's tribute to his mother."

"Was there money left over?" Emma asked.

"A few dollars, but folks seemed to order more when they found out the cause," I admitted.

"Then carry it over for tomorrow and don't worry about today, unless you want to stuff it into our tip jar," she added with a grin.

"I'll set it aside in an envelope," I told her, laughing a bit.

"Yeah, that's better," she said. "Anyway, may I?"

"You may," I told her. "Enjoy your day off tomorrow."

"You know I will," she said, but then she stopped before she left Donut Hearts. "Suzanne, if there are other things you need to be doing, Mom and I would always be happy to cover for you. All you have to do is ask."

"Thanks," I said, "but I've got it covered."

"Okay, but don't forget, you don't have to do this alone."

Her caring touched me. "I won't. See you in a few days."

"I'll be here," she said.

After she was gone, I was just about ready to head for the bank with my deposit even if Grace hadn't shown up yet. I knew that sometimes her schedule was fluid, and honestly, it was amazing to me how much time she had to help me investigate while holding down a full-time job of her own. I took one last lap around the kitchen, making sure that everything was buttoned up tightly, and then I flicked off the lights as I headed back out front.

Grace was standing outside the front door, frowning at me as I let her in.

"I thought you started without me," she said.

"I wouldn't do that to you," I said as I grabbed the deposit and headed right back to the door.

"You would too, and you know it."

"Maybe," was all that I would admit to, "but you're here now. Are you ready to start digging again?"

"I thought we might get a bite to eat first," she said. "Aren't you hungry?"

"Always," I told her. "Okay, we need to swing by the bank first and make my deposit, and then we can head over to the Boxcar Grill for a quick bite."

"It doesn't even have to be quick," she replied as we got into my Jeep.

"You don't sound all that keen on investigating today."

"I'm just not sure what else we can do," Grace admitted.

"Frankly, I'm not either. I have a feeling that we're missing something, something big, but I can't quite put my finger on what it might be."

"I hate when that happens," Grace said as we pulled up at the bank. "If you try to think about what it is, you'll never come up with it. Just forget it and let your mind drift and wander."

"That's the story of my life, drifting and wandering," I told her with a grin.

"Hey, welcome to the club," she answered.

"Thanks, it's nice to be a part of something bigger than I am," I answered as I made my deposit.

We scooted out of the bank and drove the short distance back toward the Boxcar Grill, but instead of pulling into Trish's parking lot, I stopped in front of Donut Hearts.

Grace looked across the street at the diner. "Do we have to walk from here?"

"Come on, it's just across the street. The exercise will do you good, and who knows, you might even work up an appetite."

"I've already *got* an appetite," she answered as we walked toward the diner.

"Then it will just get better," I countered.

"Hello, ladies. How's the investigation going?" Trish asked softly as we walked into the Boxcar Grill.

"I shouldn't be surprised the entire town is talking about it," I said. "It does kind of make it difficult to sneak up on our suspects, though."

"Suzanne Hart, you haven't been good at being sneaky your entire life. Am I right, Grace?"

"We're the ones who are good at that," she agreed.

"I'm going to go find a place to sit down," I told them. "When you two are finished talking about me, I'll be over there," I said as I pointed to an empty table.

I caught Trish glancing at Grace, who shrugged slightly, and I instantly knew that I was being a bit oversensitive. "Strike that. I'll stand right here and you can say anything you'd like."

"Feeling the pressure from the competitive world of donutmaking, Suzanne?" Trish asked me gently.

"No, but I hate not knowing what happened yesterday to Harper Wilcox and Emerson Glade."

"Is that it? It's easy, really. Harper drank poison, and Emerson almost married a tree. What else can I help you with?"

"Any idea who was responsible for either event?" I asked her.

"Come on, I can't do *everything* for you. You and Grace need to figure out at least *part* of it," she answered with a grin.

"True," I replied. "What's today's special?"

"Country fried steak, fried okra, and mashed potatoes," she said.

"I'll take it," I answered.

"Make it two," Grace echoed.

"Coming right up. Sweet tea?" she asked.

"What do you think?" I asked her.

"You've got it. You two are easy. I like that about you both."

"We like you too, for other reasons," Grace said.

"Ditto," I answered, and then Grace and I made it to the empty table I'd spotted earlier.

"This is really bugging you, isn't it?" Grace asked once we had our sweet teas.

"We're missing something, Grace. I just don't know what it might be."

"It will come in time, but while we're waiting for a flash of inspiration, it might be nice to be a little kinder to our friends."

"Was I really that bad?" I asked.

"Trish and I can take it, but if we're going to be interviewing suspects, it might be good to tone it down a notch," she answered.

Trish brought us our food, and as she put the plates down, she asked, "What are you two talking about?"

"Grace was just giving me a lesson in civility," I said. "Wow, that looks amazing."

"I'll tell Hilda you said so. She went back to an old favorite after the goulash disaster yesterday," she answered before turning to Grace. "Really? Since when did you start giving lectures to anybody?"

"It's something new I'm trying," Grace said as she popped a fried okra bite into her mouth. "I know these things are bad for me, but they are addicting."

"Hey, okra's a vegetable," Trish countered.

"Sure, but how can you tell under all of that fried batter?"

"You have to just trust that it's in there someplace," she said with a smile.

"I'll take your word for it," Grace said.

After we were finished eating, Grace turned to me and asked, "Feel any better?"

"Much," I admitted. "I still don't know what to do next, but my belly's full, and that's never a bad thing."

"Agreed," she said.

"So, now that we've been fed, what's next?"

"I'd like to go see Momma, if you don't mind," I told her.

"Getting a little motherly advice or hoping to score some dessert?" she asked me with a wicked smile.

"Is there something that says it can't be both?" I asked her, laughing. "I happen to know that she's working from home today, since her assistant is taking a personal day."

"Wow, Geneva gets those working for your mother?" Grace asked as we paid our checks and headed across the street back to my Jeep.

"Evidently," I said.

"Good to know," Grace said.

Before I started the engine, I got out my phone and called Momma's number. "Hey, do you have a second?" I asked her when she picked up.

"I have at least that," she admitted. "Do you want to come by for some lunch?"

"Actually, we just ate at the Boxcar," I admitted.

"Surely you have some room for some cobbler. I just made a fresh batch of peach, and if my dear sweet husband has left any, you're welcome to the crumbs."

"I heard that," Phillip said in the background.

"You were meant to," she replied to him before addressing me again. "See you soon."

"What do you want to discuss with your mother?" Grace asked me after I hung up.

"She clearly has some reservations about Harper, and I want to ask her about them. Besides, I've got an inkling, and I want to see if I might be right," I told her. "It's a long shot, but why not try?"

"True, and at the very least, we get peach cobbler," Grace answered happily.

"I'm smarter than I look," I said, and before Grace could answer, I added, "Thank goodness."

"Hey, that's my line," she protested.

"Don't worry. I'll save it for you next time."

As we drove to Momma's, I spent the time thinking about how to phrase what I wanted to ask her. Grace could obviously see that I was deep in thought, and she respected the silence as we drove the short distance to Momma's place.

By the time we got there, I had a handle on what I wanted to know.

I just hoped Momma knew the answer, or just as good, how to find it.

Chapter 19

"WOW, THAT COBBLER WAS amazing," I told Momma after I finished my serving.

"We have more if you'd like," she offered.

"Come on, Dot, the girl has to be full. Don't force her," my stepfather said.

"Phillip, stop hoarding the treats," she admonished him.

"Hey, I'm just looking out for your daughter," Phillip said as he polished off the bit of cobbler that was left in his bowl.

"You didn't have to have thirds," Momma reminded him as she transferred what was left into a container.

"I had to be a good host, didn't I?"

Grace laughed. "I, for one, am grateful that you shared any of it with us."

"You two, of course. Anyone else, they'd better bring a bat if they think they're getting any."

"Even Jake?" I asked him.

"I'll make an exception for him too, but no one else. After all, a man has to draw the line somewhere, doesn't he?"

Momma leaned over and kissed the top of his head. "You're one of a kind. You know that, don't you?"

"I do my best," Phillip acknowledged. "Now if you ladies will excuse me, I've got to make a quick phone call."

"You're welcome to stay," I told him. "In fact, we could use your opinion about something."

"So this isn't girl talk?" he asked.

"What does that mean? Girl talk? Did we go back to the fifties somehow without me knowing it?" I asked him.

"Come on, give me a break. I was just trying to be nice," Phillip said contritely.

"You are, but this is about two attempted murders in the same few hours," I said.

"You're tying in what happened with Emerson Glade and Harper Wilcox?" Momma asked us.

"We, or more precisely, Suzanne, think they are connected," Grace explained.

"But you don't think so?" Momma asked her as she continued cleaning up.

"I wouldn't say that. I just don't know," Grace admitted.

"Neither do I, truth be told," I replied. "It just seems like too big a coincidence to swallow if you know what I mean."

"I agree," Phillip said before quickly adding, "No offense, Grace."

"None taken. I defer to Suzanne enough to know that her instincts are usually solid. I just have a hard time believing that someone would run Emerson off the road and then, a few hours later, poison Harper. They just seem so different, don't they?"

"Yes," Phillip answered, "most murderers like to stick to one method, but actually, that's how a lot of them end up getting caught. One is never a pattern, but as few as two events can tell you volumes about who you're dealing with."

"How did you get to be such a good crime buster?" I asked him.

"Are you mocking me, child?" he asked.

"No, sir. It was a legitimate question. Either you've gotten better at this since you retired as the chief of police, or I'm just growing to appreciate your skills more."

Momma shrugged. "Why can't it be a little of both?"

"It can," I said. "So what do you two think? Are we barking up the wrong tree by trying to find links between the two men besides the fact that they partner on a lot of ventures together?"

"It makes sense to me," Momma said. "After all, we've seen what greed can do to folks who are usually quite reasonable. I can make some inquiries."

"That would be great," I told her.

"Suzanne, we've said from the beginning that the two main causes for someone to kill are love and money," Grace added. "What if it has nothing to do with money?"

"Well, I doubt this case has anything to do with love," I said.

"Don't forget Deidra Lang getting brushed off the day before the attempt on her boss's life," she reminded me.

"What's that all about?" Momma asked. After I explained what Deidra had experienced, she replied, "I can see her wanting to run him off the road. I've felt that way about the man myself in the past, and I have absolutely no romantic interest in him."

"That's good to know," Phillip said, sounding a bit put off.

"Don't pout. I just said I wasn't interested in him, didn't I?"

"You did," he replied. "I should take that as a win and let it go, shouldn't I?"

"That's what I would do," I admitted.

"Then that's what I'll do," he answered. "Does Deidra have feelings for Harper?"

"I don't think that's possible, but even if she did, she'd go after Gabby and not Harper, wouldn't she?" Grace asked.

"Are we sure that she didn't?" I asked.

"What do you mean?" Momma put forward.

"Gabby was standing right beside Harper when he drank that poisoned drink. Can we be sure it wasn't meant for her?"

"No, I don't suppose we can," Grace admitted. "But again, why?"

"If Deidra didn't think she could have Emerson, there was another powerful and rich man around. Getting rid of Gabby would make the way clear for her," I said.

"Suzanne, you should run this theory by Jake, or better yet, the chief," Phillip suggested.

"It's just a theory," I explained.

"Tell him that too, but it's something he should consider," the former police chief said.

"You call him, Grace," I suggested.

"Do you honestly think he'd want to hear that from me?" she asked me. "No, thank you. We're having enough communication issues as it is."

"You call him then, Phillip," I prodded.

"I'd be happy to, but it wasn't my idea."

"Fine, I'll call, but I'm putting it on speaker. We can all take the credit if we're right or the blame if we're wrong," I said as I dialed Chief Grant's number.

"What's up, Suzanne? Make it dance, I'm in a bit of a pinch."

"Have you considered Deidra Lang as a suspect?" I asked him. "I'm here with your wife, my mother, and her husband, and we're wondering if we might be on to something."

"I thought about it, investigated it, and then discarded it," the current police chief said.

"Why is that?"

"Deidra wasn't anywhere near the wedding or her boss yesterday at the crucial times," he said. "We were able to confirm her alibi."

"I know she claimed to be taking care of the paperwork for new insurance policies for everyone with Nicholas Southerland, but that might not have taken the entire morning," I suggested.

"It didn't, but it took most of it. She spent the rest of the morning trying to get her car out of the impound lot."

"I didn't hear about that," I said.

"Evidently, the chief of police in Union Square has an overly enthusiastic new cop on his roster. He spent all morning patrolling around, having cars towed for the slightest reason, including unpaid parking tickets. It took Deidra hours to get hers out of the impoundment lot, so she's in the clear."

I felt the theory of a spurned and hopeful lover die like the embers of a fire in a rainstorm. "Okay, we obviously didn't know that," I told him. "Sorry to bother you."

"It's no bother," he said, and then louder, he added, "I mean that, everyone. We'll take all the help we can get on this. Now I've got to go."

We all said our good-byes, but he was already off the phone by the time we were finished.

"So then that leaves money," I said.

"It wasn't a bad theory, Suzanne," Grace said as she tried to comfort me.

"Even if it wasn't the right one," I admitted. "Who had anything to gain financially by the dual murders of Harper and Emerson?" I turned to my mother. "Momma? Do you have any ideas?"

"Perhaps the spark of one," she admitted. "I'm assuming that Gabby didn't poison her new husband and that he didn't try to poison her."

"I can concede those points," I said.

"That leaves Emerson," Phillip said. "He and Harper took out the same kind of insurance policies on each other that Harper and Gabby did, correct?"

"That's what we've heard," I admitted.

"Okay, what if Emerson tried to poison Harper? No, he wrecked well before the poisoning happened. Could he have had a confederate do it for him?"

"I suppose it's possible," I conceded. "Momma, you have reservations about Harper, but you've never told me what they were. Care to share now?"

"It's just that he's cut a lot of corners over the years and made more than his fair share of enemies. Honestly, the pool of people who wanted to see him dead could be much wider than you've considered so far."

"Maybe so, but that still doesn't mean that his life isn't in danger, even if it's from someone we haven't considered," I said.

"I wouldn't wait a long time to find out," Phillip said. "Chances are whoever did it is going to try again, especially if he's after both men. While they are in the hospital, they both have targets on their backs. Harper Wilcox isn't safe until the person who tried to kill him is behind bars. I understand Jake was watching him last night, but who's watching him now? Just because it's daylight, it doesn't mean that the killer won't try to take another shot at it."

I grabbed my keys. "Come on, Grace. Let's go back to the hospital and talk to Harper and Gabby."

"Should we call the police chief?" Momma asked.

"No. We just gave him one bad theory. Let's not muddy the water with another. I want to see if Harper has been able to remember anything else about yesterday. Who knows? Maybe something's come back to him, or it's even possible that Gabby has been able to remember something herself. It could be that the would-be assassin has to act before either one of those things can happen!"

"At this point, I'm willing to believe just about anything," Phillip replied.

I kissed Momma's cheek on one side while Grace kissed the other. "Thanks for the dessert. We'll touch base with you later."

She was about to answer, but it was too late.

Grace and I were already on our way out the front door at a dead run.

If Phillip's theory was correct and the would-be murderer was going to strike again, we didn't have a moment to lose.

Chapter 20

WE WERE IN THE HOSPITAL parking lot when the truth hit me.

Everything that I'd learned was turned upside down, and I suddenly realized that we'd been going after the wrong person all along.

"We need to get to Gabby right now," I said as I slammed the door of the Jeep and hurried to the door.

"Why is *Gabby* in danger? Harper was the one who was poisoned," Grace said as she matched and nearly exceeded my stride.

"That's what we thought, but unless I miss my guess, Harper was behind everything." ·

"Hang on a second, Suzanne. You're not making any sense."

"We don't have time for this!" I shouted.

"We have a minute for you to explain," she said as she grabbed my arm. "We can't call Stephen with another theory until we know this time that we're right. Walk me through it."

I didn't like it, but Grace had a point. My first instinct was to call her husband and tell him my idea, but that hadn't worked out before. Maybe by telling her, I could get it all clear in my mind so I could present it to the police chief in a more cogent manner.

"The way I've worked it out, Harper is behind it all," I said. "He tried to kill Emerson, and then he tried to kill Gabby the same day. What does he get if *both* of them die?"

"Two million dollars," Grace said with a frown. "But just because he has a motive doesn't mean that he did it. If he was trying to poison Gabby, why did he almost die from it?"

"We need to ask her that," I said, "but it's not hard to believe that he spiked her drink and then somehow mixed them up."

"What about Emerson, though?" she asked.

"I'm willing to bet that if Stephen looks hard enough, he'll find one of Harper's work trucks with a scraped fender sporting red paint," I answered.

"Okay, he clearly had the opportunity and the means as well, since that poison was industrial, and both men probably had access to the chemical through one of the businesses they owned together. That still doesn't mean Harper did it. He's a rich man. Everybody in nine counties knows that."

"I think he's just like Don Smart's mother," I said, getting anxious and impatient to find my friend and protect her from her new husband.

"What does she have to do with anything?" Grace asked, looking at me with a concerned expression.

"Her son Mike thought she was rich when she died, but Don knew the truth, that she looked wealthy on the outside, but she was stone cold broke when she died."

"How sad," Grace said.

"Not at all. She lived her life to the fullest, so she invented an 'Aunt Ima' and said she was visiting her all of the time when in actuality, she was touring Europe and fulfilling her lifelong ambition. I'm guessing that Harper got himself overextended, convinced Gabby to marry him so he could insure her, and then he used that as an excuse to insure Emerson Glade, too."

"What if you're wrong, though?" Grace asked as my cell phone rang.

It was Momma. "Then I make a fool out of myself again," I said. "Hey, Momma, it's not a good time."

"This can't wait. How did you know Harper Wilcox was in debt up to his eyebrows?"

"He is?" I asked.

"I checked both men out, just as I promised you I would, and while I can't be one hundred percent certain, it appears that he's been overextended for some time. Emerson has been floating their partnership all of the cash for a few months now while Harper supposedly worked out some 'cash flow' issues of his own, but it's looking more and more like the man's completely insolvent."

"Thanks, Momma. You helped."

"Always glad to be of service," she answered as I was hanging up. I'd pay for that abruptness later, but for the moment, I had to get to Gabby.

I knew I was right this time, and even if I wasn't, the worst possibility that might happen was that she would get upset with me, an emotion I was entirely used to.

The best-case scenario was that Grace and I just might be able to save my friend's life.

Chapter 21

GABBY WASN'T IN THE ICU though, and neither was Harper.

"Where is Harper Wilcox?" I asked one of the nurses at the central station.

"He was transferred to a private room hours ago," she reported. "He's doing much better!"

"What's his room number?" Grace asked her.

"1220," she said.

"That's right beside Emerson Glade's room, isn't it?" I asked with a sinking feeling.

"Let me check." After tapping a few keys, she nodded. "That's right. He insisted we put him beside his business partner so they could be close. It's kind of sweet, isn't it?" she asked.

"Sure," I said, not bothering to stop and explain.

As we rushed to the room in question, I tried the chief's telephone. It went straight to voicemail.

"Do you know how to get ahold of Stephen?" I asked Grace as we raced down the hall.

"If he didn't answer his cell, he's either busy or he's driving," she said. "He's gotten paranoid about talking in the car lately."

"Can the chief of police just drop out of touch like that?" I asked her.

"The dispatcher can still get him on his radio, but he claims he needs a few minutes to himself every now and then just to think."

"I'll call Jake then," I said as I hit the speed dial for my husband.

It was busy.

"Listen, I'm not sure what we're going to find in there, but we can't wait for anyone else, even hospital security," I told Grace outside of the room in question.

She nodded. "I've got your back."

Before we went in, I reminded her, "He doesn't know what we know, so we just have to keep him busy until we can get some kind of backup, okay? Nobody has to be a hero."

"Sounds good to me," she said as she pulled the pepper spray from her purse and hid it in her closed fist.

We walked in, ready for a fight or a scene that would scar me for the rest of my life if he'd already acted, but that wasn't what we found.

This room was empty, too.

But then I heard voices coming from next door, and I had a hunch I knew where they all were.

Chapter 22

"I SHOULD HAVE FIGURED you two would stick your noses where they didn't belong," Harper said the moment we walked in the door.

I would have rushed him, but he had Gabby at knifepoint, so I knew if I made one sudden move, it could be the end for her.

"What did you do to her?" I asked as I pointed to Deidra Lang, slumped against the wall and clearly out of commission.

"He hit her," Gabby said in a dull, listless tone that was devoid of emotion. It appeared that she had shut down completely and was acting as though what she was experiencing was some kind of play and not real life.

"Where's Emerson?" I asked as I looked toward the bathroom.

"He's taking his laps, but he'll be here soon enough, and we can get this farce over with," Harper said.

"You're not seriously still planning on killing them both, are you?" I asked him. "Harper, we told the chief of police what you were up to. There's no way you'll get away with it now, let alone collect on both insurance policies."

"What?" Gabby asked absently. "Suzanne, what are you talking about?"

"Gabby, he rushed you into marrying him so he could insure you. Then he used that as an excuse to insure his partner as well so he could get a double payoff by killing him, too."

"But that doesn't make any sense," Gabby replied, clearly confused. "He's rich."

"Maybe on paper, but the truth is, he's flat broke." I turned to Harper and asked, "Isn't that right? Don't bother denying it. We have proof."

Harper's hand tightened on the knife at Gabby's throat as he spat out, "You had to meddle! I had it all figured out, but you messed it all up! When I tried to kill myself with that heater vent and it didn't work, I hatched a plan that was sure to succeed where I wouldn't have to die!"

"It went wrong long before we got involved," I told him. "You failed to kill Emerson when you ran him off the road, and then you poisoned yourself when you tried to kill Gabby."

"I still don't know how that happened," he snapped.

"I switched our drinks," Gabby said numbly.

"What? Why would you do that?" he asked, the fury dripping from his voice.

"You got me a Diet Coke and yourself a regular one. I heard you order them. When you turned around, I switched them."

"Why, though?"

"I wanted to help you watch your weight," Gabby said, nearly sobbing now, though no reaction showed on her face, and I doubted that she was even aware that she was crying. "That's what a good wife does."

"You nearly killed me, you fool!" he shouted.

Why was no one rushing in to help us? We certainly weren't going out of our way to keep our voices down. And where was Emerson? How many laps was the man going to take? We needed a distraction, any distraction, to get that knife away from Gabby's neck.

I reached out slowly to Grace's hand when Harper was talking to Gabby about the drinks and motioned for the pepper spray. She handed it over, much to her credit. After all, I was a bit closer to the would-be assassin than she was, so I'd have a better chance of hitting him with the debilitating spray.

The room door didn't open, but Deidra started to come to, and the second she saw what was happening, she screamed.

Harper forgot about Gabby for the moment and lunged toward Deidra to shut her up, and I had a small window in which to act.

I leapt forward and sprayed the canister into Harper's face.

There was only one problem, though.

Nothing happened.

Chapter 23

I'D FORGOTTEN THE BLASTED thing had some kind of safety on it. I couldn't figure it out at the moment, though.

There just wasn't time.

Instead of using it as a weapon one way, I decided to use it in another.

Clenching the round cylindrical container in my fist, I drove it straight into Harper Wilcox's face with every ounce of strength I had.

It didn't knock him off his feet, which was what I'd been hoping for, but it did make him stagger back, and the knife clattered to the floor at Deidra's feet.

The moment Harper recovered from my blow, he went for my throat like some kind of madman.

As his hands closed around my neck, I felt things start to get fuzzy, but the pressure suddenly eased and he staggered backward, slumped against the wall, and slid down to the floor.

There was a knife sticking in the side of his neck and a contented smile on Deidra Lang's face.

It appeared Harper Wilcox's reign of terror was over.

Chapter 24

AFTER I GOT CHECKED out in the emergency room, they decided that with the exception of some pretty nice bruises and a sore throat, I was going to be fine. Jake and Chief Grant came in together the second the examination was over.

Jake hugged me tightly, and then he pulled away. "You should have called me."

"I tried, but your line was busy," I explained.

"Then why didn't you call me?" Stephen asked.

"Your phone was off. You must have been driving," I told him.

Stephen looked as though he wanted to die. "I shouldn't have turned my ringer off. That was a stupid move. And to think I actually believed I had what it took to do your old job, Jake."

"Don't beat yourself up too badly," Jake said. "We all make mistakes."

"Yeah, but if it weren't for your wife, it could have been fatal."

"I don't deserve all of the credit," I said. "Grace had the forethought to bring the can of pepper spray in the first place, and it was my own fault I didn't know how to take the safety off. After I hit him, something in Harper seemed to snap. He would have strangled me for sure if Deidra hadn't killed him first."

"Harper didn't die," Jake said quickly.

"*That* didn't kill him?"

"Hey, if you're going to get stabbed, a hospital is the place for it to happen," Chief Grant said.

"How's Gabby? She was nearly comatose when it happened," I asked them.

"She's surely not now," Jake said. He glanced at his watch as he added, "She's probably at the courthouse right now, filing her annulment papers. Grace drove her over in your Jeep; that's the only reason she's not here right now."

"She and Grace are together?" I asked, a little surprised by the pairing.

"After what happened in Emerson's room, those two have bonded like you wouldn't believe," the chief of police said, the amusement in his voice hard to hide.

"We'll see how long that lasts," I said. "How about Emerson?"

"He's fine, since he missed all of it."

"I'd like to talk to him to confirm my theories," I said.

"Sorry, but he swept Deidra away the second he was discharged," Jake replied. "Evidently, her almost dying made him realize that he might have feelings for her after all."

"You never know, do you?" I asked. I stood and said, "If it's all the same to you gentlemen, I'd like to go home now."

"Your mother and Phillip are there waiting for you," Jake said.

"I really don't want a welcome-home party," I told him as we walked out of the emergency room together.

"They won't stay long. They just wanted to make sure you were okay, and they said something about bringing a fresh peach cobbler with them. How could I say no to that?" Jake asked with a laugh as he hugged me again.

"You couldn't," I said as I gingerly hugged him back. I turned to the chief and asked, "Do you need me for anything else?"

"You'll have to give me a formal statement later, but we're all good for now," he said. "Thanks, Suzanne."

"For what, exactly?" I asked.

"Everything. Does that cover enough ground for you?"

"Absolutely," I said.

As Jake and I drove back to our cottage, he said, "I asked Emma and Sharon to take over Donut Hearts for the next four days. Is that okay with you?"

"That's perfect. What are you going to be doing?"

As we got into his old truck, he grinned at me. "I'll be spending time with my best girl."

"Your only girl, you mean," I corrected him.

"Suzanne, I've got you. Why in the world would I ever want anyone else?"

"That's an excellent question, for which there is no answer."

As we drove, I thought about what had driven Harper Wilcox to attempt such insane actions. Money was nice, and I wouldn't turn it down if it ever fell into my lap, but I surely wouldn't let it ruin my life.

Then again, I had riches beyond a bank account in the people around me, and I knew it.

For me, that would always be more than enough.

RECIPES

Easy-as-Pie Lemon Donut Bites

Lemon is one of the favorite flavors in my house, but there are times I don't want to go to the trouble of making my tasty but labor-intensive lemon donuts, so I turn to this recipe. I usually keep a round of biscuit dough in my fridge for just such an occasion. These are easy to make, and if you eat them when they're still warm, they are an amazing lemony treat. I like lemon glaze on these as a decadent extra, and I've included that recipe below as well.

Your kids can help you cut these out, but keep them away from the hot oil!

Ingredients

1 can biscuit dough (I like Pillsbury Grands)

1 quart peanut oil for frying

Directions

Preheat your oil to 365 degrees F.

While you're waiting for the oil to come to temperature, remove the biscuit rounds from the container and form the cylinders into balls, or open the biscuits and use a donut cutter to make donut shapes.

When the oil comes to temp, add the dough cutouts or balls, being careful not to crowd the pot. Flip halfway through, about 2 to 3 minutes per side, and remove when they are golden brown on both sides.

Add the glaze below, or dust with powdered sugar, and enjoy!

Makes 4 to 8 donuts or rounds.

My Favorite Lemon Glaze

Here is an excellent recipe for a lemon glaze that's good on just about anything you can fry, bake, or make, and it couldn't be simpler!

Ingredients

¼ cup powdered confectioners' sugar

1 teaspoon whole milk (2% will do, or even water if you're out of milk)

1 teaspoon lemon juice

Optional Addition

If you have a lemon handy, use that juice for the glaze, and use a bit of zest as well! It takes this glaze to a whole new level!

Directions

Combine all ingredients in a small bowl and whisk until combined. Drizzle this mixture on top of any donut and enjoy!

My Best Peach Cobbler

I love peach cobbler, and I never hesitate to make it when I'm craving some. You can make this in peach season, but canned peaches work well too, though you don't have to tell anyone you didn't peel them yourself.

I like this recipe because it uses things I have on hand, including the canned fruit. Plus, they are easy to make and delightful to enjoy!

Ingredients

1 stick unsalted butter (1/2 cup)

1 1/2 cups granulated sugar

1 tablespoon plus 1 teaspoon cinnamon

1 cup all-purpose flour

1 1/2 teaspoons baking powder

1/2 cup whole milk (2% will do in a pinch)

1 can (29 oz.) sliced peaches in heavy syrup, drained, keeping 3/4 cup of the syrup

or fresh peaches, peeled and cut into wedges, though I've honestly had more luck with the canned peaches myself.

Directions

Preheat your oven to 360 degrees F.

While the oven is heating, melt the butter in a saucepan, then pour it into the bottom of a 9-by-13-inch pan. Set aside 1/2 cup of sugar and all of the cinnamon, and then separate the peaches from the syrup if you're using canned peaches, reserving both the peaches and the juice.

176

In a medium-sized mixing bowl, sift in 1 cup of sugar, flour, and baking powder.

Next, stir in the milk and peach syrup.

Arrange the peaches on the bottom of your dish and then pour the resulting batter over them.

Finally, mix the remaining sugar and all the cinnamon together and then sprinkle on top of the mix and bake for about an hour, or until the top is golden brown and the juices come up through the cracks in the topping. It should also pull away from the sides a bit, a sure sign that it's done.

Let cool slightly and then serve while still warm with vanilla ice cream on top.

Serves 1 if you love it as much as I do, but you could share if the mood hit you with three to five other people, though I don't recommend it!

If you enjoy Jessica Beck Mysteries and you would like to be notified when the next book is being released, please visit our website at jessicabeckmysteries.net for valuable information about Jessica's books, and sign up for her new-releases-only mail blast.

Your email address will not be shared, sold, bartered, traded, broadcast, or disclosed in any way. There will be no spam from us, just a friendly reminder when the latest book is being released, and of course, you can drop out at any time.

Other Books by Jessica Beck

The Donut Mysteries
Glazed Murder
Fatally Frosted
Sinister Sprinkles
Evil Éclairs
Tragic Toppings
Killer Crullers
Drop Dead Chocolate
Powdered Peril
Illegally Iced
Deadly Donuts
Assault and Batter
Sweet Suspects
Deep Fried Homicide
Custard Crime
Lemon Larceny
Bad Bites
Old Fashioned Crooks
Dangerous Dough
Troubled Treats
Sugar Coated Sins
Criminal Crumbs
Vanilla Vices
Raspberry Revenge
Fugitive Filling
Devil's Food Defense
Pumpkin Pleas
Floured Felonies
Mixed Malice

Tasty Trials
Baked Books
Cranberry Crimes
Boston Cream Bribes
Cherry Filled Charges
Scary Sweets
Cocoa Crush
Pastry Penalties
Apple Stuffed Alibies
Perjury Proof
Caramel Canvas
Dark Drizzles
Counterfeit Confections
Measured Mayhem
Blended Bribes
Sifted Sentences
Dusted Discoveries
Nasty Knead
Rigged Rising
Donut Despair
Whisked Warnings
Baker's Burden
Battered Bluff
The Hole Truth
Donut Disturb
Wicked Wedding Donuts
The Classic Diner Mysteries
A Chili Death
A Deadly Beef
A Killer Cake
A Baked Ham
A Bad Egg

A Real Pickle
A Burned Biscuit
The Ghost Cat Cozy Mysteries
Ghost Cat: Midnight Paws
Ghost Cat 2: Bid for Midnight
The Cast Iron Cooking Mysteries
Cast Iron Will
Cast Iron Conviction
Cast Iron Alibi
Cast Iron Motive
Cast Iron Suspicion
Nonfiction
The Donut Mysteries Cookbook

47594382R00104